Lakota Dreams

Tina Velazquez

PublishAmerica
Baltimore

© 2009 by Tina Velazquez.
All rights reserved. No part of this book may be reproduced, stored in a retrieval system or transmitted in any form or by any means without the prior written permission of the publishers, except by a reviewer who may quote brief passages in a review to be printed in a newspaper, magazine or journal.

First printing

All characters in this book are fictitious, and any resemblance to real persons, living or dead, is coincidental.

PublishAmerica has allowed this work to remain exactly as the author intended, verbatim, without editorial input.

ISBN: 978-1-60749-638-0 (softcover)
ISBN: 978-1-4489-0918-6 (hardcover)
PUBLISHED BY PUBLISHAMERICA, LLLP
www.publishamerica.com
Baltimore

Printed in the United States of America

This book is dedicated to The International Wolf Foundation of Ely, Minnesota. Thank you so much for taking care of and educating people about God's amazing animals, wolves. It is also dedicated to the people of The Pine Ridge Reservation. Always keep your heritage alive and don't let anyone ever take your beliefs away from you. I ask that anyone who appreciates wolves or the Native American heritage make a donation to either of the above. May God (The Great Spirit) be with you all.

Lakota Dreams

1

Spirit of Greywolf lived a very simple life in the Black Hills of South Dakota. Simple…until the day he began having vivid dreams of a beautiful red-haired woman. Every time he went to sleep this woman would appear. But who was she? And would he ever meet her. Deep inside he felt this must be a sign from The Great Spirit. He knew that one day he would meet this woman and they would fall in love.

Kiara had just moved to South Dakota from Minnesota where she had been raising wolves. She made a living for herself by traveling to Native American Reservation events called *Pow Wows*, where she educated people about wolves and sold Black Hills Gold jewelry. She attended her first Pow Wow right outside of The Pine Ridge Reservation. Her eyes were immediately drawn to a Native American man who took her breath away. Who was this man, she wondered, and would she ever be able to meet him?

The air was finally starting to warm up after what seemed like a very long winter. Living in South Dakota, the winters could sometimes be brutal with snow and cold. Kiara had moved here from Minnesota about four months ago with her eight wolves.

Minnesota winters could be the same though, so she was used to it. Kiara's name came from her Irish heritage, meaning dark, feminine of Ciaran. It was the name of a saint who had deep red hair that fell half way down her back and the bluest of eyes like a pool of water. Kiara's attention was suddenly distracted by two of the wolves roughhousing outside. "Dakota and Denali stop that, you two goofs," Kiara yelled.

Every morning, Kiara got up early and, before even having her morning coffee, she went out the door to tend to her babies. She raised Timber Wolves that she brought to Native American Pow Wow's so that she could educate people about these magnificent animals. Over the last four years, she has been raising eight wolves, four males and four females. Dakota was one of the males and Denali was a female. Kiara was pretty sure they would be wolf parents soon. They had mated over the winter and soon would have pups, but that didn't stop their playfulness with each other.

Kiara purchased an old farmhouse with ten acres of land when she moved to South Dakota. She had someone put up a huge pen around three big trees and even had him build a small house. Kiara spent more time out there with the wolves than she did in her own house. Over the years it was as if they had become one.

Kiara heard a horn and turned around to see Dr. Eagle. He was there to check on how Denali was coming along.

"Hey Kiara, how's our little mama doing?"

"She seems to be doing good. I can't get her to quit running around all the time though."

"That's okay, it's not going to hurt her."

They walked over to where Dakota and Denali were laying on the ground under a tree. Dr. Eagle checked her out while speaking softly to her to keep her calm.

"She's doing great," he said. "I'm still going with the dates I gave you. Anytime between April 14th and April 18th."

It took fifty-nine to sixty three days for wolf pups to be born and I figured Denali had conceived on Valentine's Day. The week prior, her and Dakota were nuzzling a lot, which is what wolves do before mating. When wolves mate, it is usually for life.

"Well we have at least ten days to go then." Kiara said to Dr. Eagle.

"That would be about right, Kiara. Take care of her now and call if you need me."

"Oh I will. Thanks Doc."

I waved as Dr. Eagle pulled away and went back to feed her babies. Then I went into the house as they ate to finally have my morning coffee. I had to make a few calls today to finalize my participation at a Pow Wow coming up in May, outside of the Pine Ridge Reservation. Dr. Eagle was kind enough to tell me he'd take care of the wolves while I was gone, since I was only taking Chinook, Maheegan and Makala. The pups would be born by then and I didn't want to leave them alone, even though wolves can take care of themselves. I felt much better knowing someone would be there with them.

2

Spirit of Greywolf went outside of his teepee to start a morning fire. He was awakened early again today by the same dream of the red-haired woman. He wondered why he kept having the reoccurring dream. It had been going on for months now and he was certain he had never met this white women. Spirit of Greywolf's skin was of a bronze color and he had jet-black hair almost to his waist. He usually had it braided, but today he hadn't done that yet. His bulging muscles glistened in the morning sunshine.

He went over to say hello to his two Palominos, Sunshine and Runs Like The Wind. They saw him coming and trotted over to greet him. "Wanka Tanka bless you today." (*Wanka Tanka* translates to God.) Spirit of Greywolf's horses were his life. They traveled with him throughout the Pow Wow circuit.

"It's been many moons since we have been to a Pow Wow my little ones. Next month we will be going to one right down the road. It is time for the Pow Wow season to begin."

Most Pow Wows were between April and November. This year, the first one would be in May, right outside of The Pine

LAKOTA DREAMS

Ridge Reservation. Spirit of Greywolf didn't live far from there. There would be much singing and dancing. Spirit of Greywolf went back to his fire to make some frybread. He was proud of his Native American heritage, of being a Lakota, as he should be. He was always one of the main dancers at the Pow Wows and most always won prize money in the competition. He thanked Wanka Tanka for his life and his food before eating.

3

Kiara went into town to pick up some groceries. She had to be at the library at two o'clock to give a speech to a group of school children about wolves. She always brought one of her wolves with her for the children to meet. Today she decided she'd bring Maheegan. The wolf was in a trailer being pulled by her truck. The children were always fascinated when they met a real wolf.

Kiara always started out her speech by telling the children about how wolves are not like the wolf in Little Red Riding Hood. She most always had a good reaction to that, since the little children always seemed to think the wolf was going to eat them when she brought them into the room on a leash. Today the children were from a local first grade class, so it should be fun. They were young enough to appreciate the beauty of the wolf.

Next week was going to be a first for Kiara. She was going to a nursing home in town. She hoped the residents would like what she had to say. She went into the store and picked up what she needed and headed over to the library. When she got there the bus was already in the parking lot, which meant the children were already in the building. She pulled around the back door and

Dana, one of the young girls that worked at the library with the school trips, opened the door.

"Hey Kiara, how's it going today? How's Denali doing? Pretty soon for the pups right?"

"Yeah, Dr. Eagle was there today and said she's doing fine. About another ten to fifteen days. I'm so excited. These will be the first pups born to one of my wolves. I'm nervous too though, that's why I'm glad he'll only be a phone call away when the time comes. The kids are already here, right?"

"Yep! They arrived about fifteen minutes ago."

"Okay then, lets get this show on the road."

Kiara and Dana walked into the room where all the children were anxiously awaiting her arrival. Dana always helped Kiara since she was in charge of the library events. She came up with an idea to bring in Boy Scout Troops one day and Girl Scouts another. So next week, Kiara would be back with one of the wolves again. She usually only came once a month, but now she'd be coming twice.

"Hi kids," she said as she entered the room.

"Where's the wolves?" they all started shouting.

"Well first I have to teach you a little about wolves, then I'll bring one out and you'll be able to see her. Her name is Maheegan. Now, you won't be able to pet her. You'll only be able to look at her, but if you come back in about three months I'll have a surprise for you. I'll be bringing some wolf pups and you'll be able to hold and feed them with a bottle." The children all started clapping. "Okay now lets start learning about wolves."

Kiara began by explaining to the children that there was always an Alpha wolf to every pack. She then went on to explain just about everything the children could ever need to know about wolves! They were very excited with all they were learning!

Kiara finally brought out Maheegan to meet the children. They all loved her and appreciated her more now because they knew so much about wolves. Before Kiara knew it, her time was over.

"Okay Dana, see you next week!"

"Yep, I'll see you then! Take care," Dana waved. "Call me if Denali has the pups."

4

Spirit of Greywolf was traveling to see his parents, Chance Two Bears and Lori Rain Showers. Chance Two Bears was a Spirit Warrior and his mother, Lori Rain Showers was a dancer in the Pow Wows in the Jingle Dress category.

"Pretty soon our first Pow Wow of the year will be upon us," Spirit of Greywolf said.

"Ai, it won't be long," his father said.

"Well I need to go get firewood so I stopped to see if you need any."

"We're fine," Lori Rain Showers said.

Spirit of Greywolf left to gather firewood. He lived in The Black Hills right outside of The Pine Ridge Reservation in South Dakota. His lifestyle was very simple. He owned about 20 acres of land where he built his teepee and lived very comfortably. He had a huge corral for his two prized horses. All his cooking was done outside. He lived a very rural life, as did his ancestors. He was very proud of his Lakota Heritage and the ways of his people. He had been traveling the Pow Wow circuit since he was twelve years old with his parents. Over the winter, his horses had mated and it wouldn't be long before he'd welcome a new colt to the family. He was looking forward to that. He started thinking again about that dream he kept having. Who was this red haired woman? It seemed like she was some kind of vision to him. There had to be some kind of meaning to it. He just didn't know what it was.

5

Kiara had one more stop she had to make on the way home. She had to go pick up her order of Black Hills Gold Jewelry that she sold at Pow Wows. She had a simple way of life since she moved to South Dakota. As long as she was with her wolves and had enough money to pay her bills and take care of them from her income of selling her jewelry she was happy. She was so involved with the raising of her wolves. There was no one special in her life and never really was. She was very content, though. Although she had to admit, when she watched her wolves at play, she sometimes wished she had someone to share her days and nights with. To have that closeness and the loving strong arms of a man around her would be nice. But the thought always left her mind as fast as it came into it. Really…what man would want to be with wolves and have them as such a huge part of their life? What man would want to have such a simple life where not much money was made? None that she knew of, not that she was looking. Oh well… I have my babies and that's all that really matters

6

Spirit of Greywolf's body glistened in the afternoon sun as his muscles showed he was working hard. Since planting season was right around the corner and he grew all his own vegetables he was plowing a section of his land to grow corn. He wiped at his forehead as beads of sweat were forming. He was naked from the waist up, his pectoral muscles were flexed with hard work and he had beads of sweat forming on his chest. I should sleep well tonight, he thought. Maybe that red-haired woman won't invade my dreams.

When he was done, he went down to the stream and washed up. Then he went back to the corral and checked on his horses before going to start a fire. He was making Indian Tacos tonight, one of his favorite foods. By then it would be time to retire for the night.

7

Kiara was excited for the day, especially since she took care of most of her errands yesterday. She supposed she would start going through the shipment of jewelry she picked up yesterday. The wolves have all been taken care of already and she was enjoying her morning coffee. She started unpacking the jewelry on the kitchen table and noticed there were some beautiful items. She almost hated to sell it, but it helped pay the bills.

When she was done sorting the new jewelry, she went outside and sat under the umbrella table watching the wolves. Dakota and Denali were curled up together sleeping under one of the trees. Makala and Mingan were chasing each other around the yard. Chinook and Mohegan were playing tug of war with a big rope that they found on the ground. Maheegan and Shunkaha were just sitting watching the four like they were crazy. She smiled as she watched them and realized what a big part of her life they had become and how lonely she'd be without them. Pretty soon she'd have five more, according to Dr. Eagle. It was getting late and her babies were all starting to settle in for the night, so she went into the house to go to sleep.

8

She was riding bareback on a black horse. Her long flowing red hair flew behind her as she rode. She rode right past him and he could see her face. She smiled at him and kept going. He watched her as she turned back and waved.

Spirit of Greywolf woke with a start. There it was again. The dream of this red haired woman. Who was she and what did this mean? Spirit of Greywolf walked out of his teepee and started a fire. The air was crisp this morning. He shook his head to try to get that dream out of his head. He needed to go talk to one of the elders on the reservation to see if he knew what it could mean. After he had his fry bread he would go. He knew exactly who he would go see, Wild Running Horse. He was a spiritual leader and he also knew about dreams.

"Spirit of Greywolf how are you? I haven't seen you in months," said Wild Running Horse.

"I'm fine. Glad winter is finally over. I came because I need your help on the meaning of a dream I keep having."

"What is it? I will surely help you if I can."

He told him about the red-haired woman.

"I believe this means there is a woman somewhere in your future. It is about time you have a female to share your life with you."

"Where will I meet this woman? I don't even know any white women," I said.

"That is yet to be seen. How do we ever know when or where we will meet someone? It is in Wanka Tanka the eye of our beholder. It will happen though. It is in the stars. You will teach her the ways of The Lakota because you are very true to your heritage. You are very proud and you live a simple life."

"I thank you. My life is a little lonely. Maybe this woman is whom Wanka Tanka wants me to be with. I will have to keep my eyes wide open," said Spirit of Greywolf.

9

"Dr. Eagle its me, Kiara. I think it's time. Denali is acting strange. I went out this morning to feed her and she was panting and walking back and forth. Dakota won't leave her side either. It is April 16th so she's right on schedule. Would you be able to come and see? I'm so nervous!"

"Of course, I could get there within the hour. Don't panic. She knows what to do. Everything will be fine. Just sit outside of the pen and watch her."

She hung up the phone and went back outside to sit at the table and watch Denali. She didn't want to get too close, because she really didn't know how Denali would react. She hoped the doc would make it here soon.

Exactly an hour had passed, and here came Dr. Eagle.

"How's she doing?" he asked.

"About the same, but she just went behind the tree and laid down about twenty minutes ago."

"Well let me go take a look."

I watched as he went. I didn't want to go in the pen with him because I didn't want to get her upset. He came out and smiled.

"Well come on and see! You're the proud Grandma of 5 beautiful gray pups."

"Oh," I came running and crying at the same time. "Are you sure? I won't upset her?"

"No, of course not."

We went into the pen and there was Denali with 5 pups and Dakota by her side. "Oh my, they are beautiful." They were all nestled by Denali, who was lying on her side. It was the most beautiful thing she had ever seen. She had tears in her eyes. "Oh Denali you did good. They are beautiful. Dakota you too!"

"Well they look healthy, Kiara, and Denali looks good too. Now all you have to do is think of 5 names. You have 3 girls and 2 boys. Don't worry about them too much though. She'll take good care of them. She knows what to do, and when they get a little bigger the whole pack will help her. Just try to give her a little extra food to make up for what she gives the pups. Call me if you need me."

"Thanks doc, I'm so glad you were here. I was so nervous!"

"You did fine," he said.

Kiara sat down at the table to watch the wolves. She couldn't really see the pups since they were behind the tree with Dakota and Denali. The other wolves didn't seem to bother them. They were doing their own thing and playing with each other. Kiara went into the house to have something to eat. It had been a very exciting morning and she didn't feel much like eating, so she just made herself a small sandwich.

10

What a shocker it was when Spirit of Greywolf went out to the corral. Instead of two horses, there were two horses and a brand new colt! Sometime in the night, Sunshine had given birth.

"I see your beautiful colt. I am proud of you two. I see it is a boy. What name will we give him? I know, Comes At Night since that is when he was born." Spirit of Greywolf gave each one of them an apple and threw in some hay and changed their water. He went to have his morning frybread and coffee. He had nothing to do today except plant his corn seeds, so he was just going to lay outside of his teepee for a while and watch the new arrival and his parents. As he was lying there, he decided to paint a picture of a wolf on the canvas of his teepee on one side and a pony on the other. He's always loved wolves and he also wanted to honor the new colt that had arrived that night.

He sat on the ground and picked up his brushes to start to paint. After a few hours, he had painted two beautiful pictures. He sat back looking at them and was very satisfied.

11

The next day Kiara got up and went right outside to tend to the wolves and check on the pups. She had slept really well the night before. She was exhausted from the exciting day she had. When she got out there, Dakota and Denali were under the same tree as yesterday. Denali was feeding the pups and Dakota was just sitting there watching. I still couldn't believe she had five pups! This was the first litter I ever had. I had gotten all my wolves as pups, so they were all fairly young yet.

Dakota and Denali were the Alpha and the Beta of the pack. The Alpha, Dakota, was the highest-ranking wolf within the dominance hierarchy and Denali, the Beta, was the second ranking wolf. They were the leaders for sure! They had always been close since I brought them home within a week of each other. They were also the ones I was closest to, probably because they were my first wolves. After all, they were one of God's greatest creations. Who couldn't love them? They are so beautiful, I thought as I stood there looking at all of them. I couldn't believe there were actually people who hunted and killed these animals. I would do whatever I had to if it ever came to protecting mine. I put out their food as they all ran up to greet me, wagging their tails. Chinook was showing me his teeth as usual, like he was smiling at me. He always made me laugh. I guess he was a favorite too! Who was I kidding? They were all my favorites. They each had their own unique. Maheegan was the shyest one. I believe she was considered the Omega, which meant she was the lowest ranking wolf. She was a sweetheart. Her name in the Native American language meant "grey wolf." Makala, a female, always seemed to be getting into some sort of mischief. Shunkala, a male whose name meant "wolf," was also shy. I'd say he was the biggest baby of them all too!

When I went in last night, I had thought a lot about what Dr. Eagle had said about picking out names. I sat in the house trying to think of five names. Five names...one is hard enough, but five? I got out a piece of paper and wrote ideas down. I thought of name after name. I decided on naming one of the girls Calin, which in my Irish heritage meant "girl." Next I decided on Kayla for the second girl and Casey for the last girl. Now for the boy's names. I thought of the Pow Wows I had participated in and the tribe of Native Americans that fascinated me the most, the Lakotas. Maybe that's why I had moved to South Dakota, to learn more about them and their heritage. I decided on Misum, which is pronounced (Mee soon) which means "Little brother" in the Lakota language. Finally for the last one, I picked Tacoma, which was also the name of the truck I drove. I wondered what different markings they had so I'd be able to tell them apart.

The one I decided to name Tacoma was all black like Chinook, so that would be easy. The rest were all gray though, so I'd have to remember their different markings. When they got to be a few months old, they'd all have their own personalities so I'd figure out who was who quickly.

"Well since I named them all I guess I'm keeping them all!" I started laughing because I knew all along that I'd keep every one of them. "Wow," I said, realizing I had thirteen wolves. My dream four years ago was to someday own a wolf. I would never have thought that I'd ever have thirteen. What if Maheegan and Shunkaha were to have pups? They were really close too! Boy I better start selling a lot of Black Hills Gold, I smiled. I wouldn't trade this life for anything. This was a dream come true for me!

I watched as all the wolves ate their food and played. The pups were all running around and chasing each other. They were so small that they looked like little rabbits. Who couldn't love this, I thought? Dakota was licking Denali and as usual Makala and Maheegan, the mischievous ones were digging a hole by the tree. I could sit here and watch them all day, but I needed to get in the house and do some work. I waved to them and told them I'd be back later. Not that they notice much…they were all having too much fun!

12

    Spirit of Greywolf was out in the corral with the colt and the proud new parents. He watched the new colt with pride in his eyes.
    Again last night he had the dream of the white woman. Strangely though, this time she had a wolf with her. She was walking towards him, but before she reached him, he woke up. He lay in bed for a while thinking of this woman. He looked around his teepee and looked at all the dream catchers he had. Because this dream occurred every night, he had started to long for this woman whom he didn't even know. He wanted to meet her. He wanted to run his fingers through her long red hair. He wanted to caress her smooth body, and kiss her succulent lips. He felt a stir beneath his sheets. I must stop thinking of this woman, he thought.
    He walked over to his truck to get out the hay he had picked up yesterday. He lifted down the gate, which had two bumper stickers on it. One said "Indian Power—Lakota Pride" and the other said "My Lakota People—Nothing is Forgotten—Only Left Behind." He had great respect for his heritage and for his people.

13

Kiara went into town early with Chinook and Maheegan. She had an event today at the library with the boy scouts. As usual, Dana was at the back door to greet her.

"Whom do we have today?" she asked.

"Oh, I decided on Chinook for the boy scouts. I thought they'd love his black fur."

"Great, they're here already, so whenever you want to start."

"Okay, lets get this show on the road," Kiara said.

She brought Chinook in and went to introduce him to the scouts and tell them the same speech about wolves she always did. She had been right too. When she brought Chinook in she could tell the boys really loved him and his color.

Before she knew it, her time was up and it was time to part again. Dana walked her to the door as usual.

"Until next week," she said.

"Yeah, I'm heading over to the nursing home. I have a few hours with them today. This is a first time there so I hope it goes well."

"Good luck! I'm sure it will. It's always been a hit here," Dana said.

TINA VELAZQUEZ

As she pulled up to the nursing home, one of the aides was outside with a few of the residents. She told her to pull around the back. Kiara pulled around to the back and a woman let her in.

"Hi, I'm Kiara," I said.

"Hi, I'm Ann. I'll be helping you. I'm so excited about this. I think this will be really good for a lot of our residents."

"Me too, I hope it goes well. I've been looking forward to this all week. I'm hoping that this program helps some of your residents too. I'm sure some of them are lonely. I'll be back in with my wolf. I brought Maheegan with me today. She is my shyest wolf, so I knew she'd be good with the residents here. I'll start out by telling them a little about wolves first, but I think they'd like to see her as I'm telling them."

14

She was sitting at the edge of the lake. He saw the sun shining on her long red hair. To him, she was a vision of beauty. He was mesmerized by her looks. It looked as though she was deep in thought. Her back was against a tree and her head was tilted toward the sun with her eyes closed. He approached her very quietly. She looked up as he came toward her and the sun on her face was blocked. He reached out his hand to her. As she took it, he pulled her up and took her in his arms. He hugged her tightly and kissed her head. "Techihhila," (which meant *I love you*). She lightly pulled away and said I love you too, Spirit of Greywolf. They kissed deeply as he rubbed her back and drew his hands through her hair. "My life was nothing before you. You are now my woman."

They kissed deeply again as he cupped her bosom and she melted into his arms. He laid her on the ground ever so gently as he rained small kisses all over her face and neck. He pulled his fingers through her long red hair. She met his kiss with her own and twirled his long dark hair.

"Where have you been all my life, Spirit of Greywolf?"

"I am here now Kiara. I am here now and always for you. You are my woman. You will become my wife, my *mitawin*. You will become one with me. You will become a Lakota."

She could feel his pants starting to swell. His kisses were becoming urgent. His tongue slid deeply into her mouth.

"Kiara, oh Kiara my woman, my *winyan*" (this in Lakota meant woman).

He woke with a start. There were beads of sweat all over his body. "Wanka Tanka help me. This is only a dream, but who is this woman, this woman that I long for? Please bring her into my life."

Spirit of Greywolf shook his head as he tried to clear the dream he had just had again. He needed to meet this woman. He needed to know who she was. He believed she was whom he was to spend the rest of his life with. She was his other half, the missing piece of the puzzle. Where was he to meet her? This woman that he had never even met, but he already knew he loved. She was being sent from the heavens. She was in his dreams nightly. This was a message he kept getting.

He went outside to tend to his horses, but before going to the corral he started a fire and put his coffee on. He got to the corral and Comes At Night, his new colt came running up. He nuzzled Spirit of Greywolf's hand as if to say hello. Spirit of Greywolf patted the top of his head and spoke softly to him. Then walked over Sunshine and Runs Like the Wind. He went into the corral and filled their water and made sure they had enough food. Then he led Runs Like the Wind out of the corral and jumped on his back. He always rode bareback. It was the Lakota way. He didn't believe in a saddle.

He rode for about a half hour, knowing that no matter what he did he wouldn't be able to clear his head of that woman. Even now in his wakened state he could picture her, her flaming red hair and her blue eyes looking into his. Her perky breasts filling out the shirt she had on. The smile on her face was only meant for him.

He rode faster back to the corral with a crazy thought that this woman would be there next to the fire, tending to their coffee. "One day I will meet this woman. I will make her mine. I've had a vision and she will lie with me and become my mitawin."

"Wahi," Spirit of Greywolf shouted to his horses. He sat down by his fire and had his coffee, but then quickly got up and started dancing. "Ha-ay-hee-ee, Ha-ay-hee-ee," he kept chanting, which was a call to the Great Spirit. A call to Wanka Tanka. He decided he would go see his *Ate* (which meant father) and his *Ina* (which meant mother).

Ai. Even though Spirit of Greywolf knew the English language, he still spoke and thought often in his native Lakota tongue. You should never forget your past and where you came from. That is what he always told the children on the reservation when he went there.

He believed the Lakota heritage could stay strong as long as everyone still believed. It was hard though, because life for the Lakota people on the Pine Ridge Reservation was hard. Eighty percent were unemployed. The average income was only $3,700 per year. The life expectancy of a man was only forty-eight years old and fifty-two years for a woman. It was sad, but Spirit of Greywolf tried to do all he could for them. His parents still lived on the reservation. That is also where Wild Running Horse lived. He would go see him today too! He made extra frybread to take to some of the children of the reservation and to his *Ate* and *Ina*.

15

Kiara was still exhausted from the day before, but she was also happy. Chinook was a hit with the boy scouts and Maheegan did pretty well too! The residents at the nursing home were as excited as the kids were to get to meet two very real wolves. They were a big hit and the residents couldn't wait for them to come back. Kiara decided to stay in today, since she had packing to do for the Pow Wow she would be leaving for in a few days. It was not far from home, but it was the opening of the Pow Wow season and she was really excited.

She hadn't been to a Pow Wow since last November, right around Thanksgiving. The pups were getting big already and Dr. Eagle was still going to be caring for them while she was gone. She was going to take Chinook, Maheegan, and Makala just as planned. The others would all get their chance over the summer months to go to other Pow Wows. She already had all her Black Hills Gold in cases and ready to go. All she needed was her clothes. She would leave the day after tomorrow in the early morning and, as usual, she always camped with her wolves. She actually loved it at night because she always camped away from everyone else, but she always made a nice campfire and made it fun for them.

She had thought about an article she read in the paper the other day about the Native American children on the Pine Ridge Reservation. There were many that needed clothes for the summer and toys. She had decided she would go and pick up some things to bring to the children. She was even going to see if one day she could bring some of the wolves to their school to educate them on wolves. But that would have to wait until she came back, since she was just so exhausted. The Pow Wow was going to be on the reservation grounds. The Pine Ridge Reservation was the second largest reservation in the United States. It was home to the Oglala Sioux Tribe. She remembered reading about some of their great leaders when she first moved out here.

There was Chief Red Cloud, who had a burial site over looking the school that was named after him called Red Cloud Indian School. That was when she learned about the children. Sioux Chief Big Foot was another one she had read about. He was another prominent Lakota leader. He led his band on a journey to flee from the U.S. Army, but their journey ended on December 28, 1890 at Wounded Knee where hundreds of Lakota people, including Chief Big Foot, were killed by the seventh cavalry. She was glad that four of the Pow Wows she would be attending were in South Dakota this year.

16

Tomorrow, Spirit of Greywolf would be leaving for his first Pow Wow of the season. He was excited. It was always a great honor to be among his people. After talking again yesterday with Wild Running Horse, he was sure that the meeting with the red-haired woman was coming closer.

In fact, he was looking forward to sleep tonight. He wanted to dream of this white woman again. He wanted to see her smiling eyes. He wanted to wrap his strong arms around her delicate body and kiss her face and lips. He decided it would be time for bed now, even though it was early. He had to see her again, even if it was only for a moment. He looked around his tipi. It was about eighteen feet tall and in the middle was a small fire with smoke going out of a hole in the top. He also had many dream catchers. The Native Americans believed that when you slept at night and dreamed, your good dreams go through the holes in the web and your bad dreams would get caught in the web. He wanted all his dreams to go through tonight. He wanted all good dreams of this *winyan*.

"Ha-ah-hee-ee," he looked up to the top of his tipi and ever so softly chanted, hoping the Great Spirit would take him to this woman again.

His chanting worked because there she was, her long red hair billowing over the front of her shoulders. She put her hand out to him and he walked over to her. He cupped her face as she slid her fingers over his face ever so gently. She lightly kissed his lips as he cupped one of her breasts in his hand. Besides in his dream, he had never been so close to any woman as he was to this woman. He helped her onto his horse and got on behind her and they rode off into the sunset together, with her long red hair flying behind her. The feel of her body was so close to him. Pressed into his chest. The scent of this woman was so powerful to him.

17

Kiara couldn't believe the beauty of the drive on the way to the reservation. There was a mixture of Ponderosa Pines dotting the land with breathtaking sand hills and craters. These people are very rich in their culture and tradition, she thought. There was a pride among their people, which was unmistakable. This was her first Pow Wow since she moved here. She remembered the very first week she was here. She had met an elder Native American man who told her about the Lakotas. He had said that the Lakota of the Great Sioux of North America had a rich spirituality and a deep respect for life, visible and invisible. He had told her that the word "Lakota" meant "Considered friends," or "Alliance of Friends."

He went on to tell her that Forever Lakota was what his people would be and that being a warrior was learning how to cry. It wasn't about strength like people thought. He had told her to be proud of her heritage and who she was.

Kiara pulled over to check on Chinook, Maheegan and Makala. She was going to be staying at a campground right outside of the reservation, but she still wanted to stop and call Dr. Eagle to make sure everyone at home was fine first.

He picked up on the second ring. "Hey doc, how are my babies?" Kiara asked.

"Well for goodness sake, you haven't even been gone that long. Are you missing them already?" he laughed. "Of course you knew I would. Well, they're all doing fine. I was just outside playing with them. The pups are getting so big already."

"I know, they grow so fast. Well, I'll call again tomorrow before the opening ceremony. I'm almost to the campground. I know I don't have to tell you this, but take good care of my babies!" Kiara felt like she was going to cry.

"You know I will. I love them as much as you do. I wouldn't let anything happen to them," Dr. Eagle said.

Kiara hung up and got back in her truck to head into the campground. She talked to the girl inside who told her how to get to her campsite. She sometimes hated bringing her wolves to the Pow Wows because she had to keep them caged the whole time. They weren't free to roam in a huge enclosure like at home. When she got to the campsite, she had time to sit and relax for the evening because the Pow Wow didn't actually start until tomorrow. She made sure all her jewelry was ready to be set up and then fed the wolves. Then she sat down to have a sandwich to eat. The weather was actually warm for this time of year, she was happy for that. It was so peaceful out here. You could see all the fires from people camping and hear the laughter, since everyone was happy to be here. Crickets were chirping in the night air. She even heard an owl hoot! Her wolves were howling ever so softly. Tomorrow would be a long day so she turned in early. Before she knew it, she was falling asleep.

18

Spirit of Greywolf was staying in his mother and father's home. The smell of sweet grass was in the air. His mother was busy cooking frybread and coffee when he came in the door.

"Yuta, Cinks," she said. Which means eat, my son.

He sat down to have some of his mother's frybread and coffee. Wild Running Horse was sitting at the table. "Spirit of Greywolf, how are you?" he asked.

"Good, very good I am excited about tomorrow's Pow Wow circuit starting up again," he said. He showed him what he had brought to wear tomorrow. It was so colorful. Red, blue, purple, green and yellow with a triangle of blue, white and yellow on the arm and number 1442 on his other arm. The band for his head was of a blue color and had feathers sticking out of it, but the best was what he would be wearing on his head. It looked like a wolves head. In their culture, the wolf is regarded as the source and patron of the hunt and of the war. Spirit of Greywolf decided that this year his costume would be of the wolf.

"You will win again this year in many Pow Wows, Spirit of Greywolf. This I am sure. Just as I am sure you will meet this

Wiwasteka (beautiful woman) that comes to you in your dreams," Wild Running Horse said.

"Ai, you are a great man of Lakota Oyate."

"Pila mita kola,"(my thanks friend) Spirit of Greywolf said.

"This woman, ai, I had dreams about her again last night. It is every night now that this winyan comes to me. I do need to find her. I will find her!"

Everyone sat in quiet as they thought about what Spirit of Greywolf said.

Spirit of Greywolf was going to be Master of Ceremonies for this year's Intertribal Pow Wow, so after The Grand Entry he would have to talk to his people. He excused himself after eating so he could think of what he would say tomorrow.

19

Kiara awoke early since she was so excited about the Pow Wows starting up again. She really wanted to get her wolves to the Pow Wow grounds early, so she put Chinook, Makala and Maheegan in the back of her truck and headed out. She would get coffee at the Pow Wow along with frybread, which was a favorite of hers at these events. She pulled up and a man named Thunder Pony was at the entrance of the grounds.

"Hohahe, kola," he said to her with a smile. This meant *welcome friend* in the Lakota language.

"Hohahe, kola," Kiara responded.

He handed her a program and told her where she would be setting up. After she got her wolves settled, she walked over to the food booths and got herself a cup of coffee and her frybread, which was already made for all the participants at the Pow Wow. She went back and sat in her chair to look at the program. The master of ceremonies for this particular Pow Wow was a Lakota named Spirit of Greywolf who grew up on the Pine Ridge Reservation and had lived here his whole life.

Greywolf, Kiara thought, I wonder what he's like? His name is like my passion for the gray wolf. I will have to make it a point to meet this man.

As usual, after the opening of the Grand Entry there would be much singing and dancing. Let's not forget though that a Pow Wow is not only a time for everyone to get together, but it has religious significance. There would be the parade of dancers: men's traditional, women's traditional, men's grass dancers, women's jingle dancers, men's fancy dancers. She noticed Spirit of Greywolf's name listed under men's fancy dance. Then there was women's fancy shawl dance and last the smallest of the girls and boys. After the Grand Entry there would be the flag song and an invocation would bless the gathering. The Eagle Staff would be positioned above the Canada flag to signify First Nation and is then tied to a pole in the center of the circle. Then Spirit of Greywolf will yell NOW WE DANCE! It is an honor among Native Americans to carry the Eagle Staff. Also, she had learned they believe Wanka Tanka, which is The Great Spirit, is the supreme power of the Lakota Universe. The Lakotas had great culture and understanding. Their Pow Wows, which really had religious significance, honored everyone. They honored their creator, and then they honored our veterans, our elders, and last but not least, our ancestors. No one was left out. Everyone was included.

As I sat there and thought about that, I realized that they were much better people than most I knew. If we went back many years, their land was taken from them and they were put on reservations, told where they had to live. And yet they survived and made something of themselves. She was startled to hear a man's voice over a speaker.

"Hohahe, (welcome) to our annual Oglala Lakota Vietnam Veterans Contest Pow Wow here at the Pine Ridge Reservation grounds. I am Spirit of Greywolf. I am here to tell you that the drumbeat that you will hear is the drumbeat of our people. As long as that is still heard we are still living! Without the drum there wouldn't be dancers. Without the heartbeat of Mother Earth the dancers can't dance. We wouldn't be here. We dance with pride! There are so many heavens, so many places to travel, but there is nothing as beautiful as our land here! I sometimes live in the valley of dreams. I don't know what they mean, but I hope someday to find out. Now though, I must invite you to our Grand Entry and LET"S POW WOW!!!!"

I couldn't take my eyes off of the bronze man that stood there speaking. So that was Spirit of Greywolf. WOW!!! He was the most gorgeous man I had ever laid my eyes on! Not only in his looks and his bulging muscles, but also with the words that came out of his mouth, the words that seemed to come from his very soul. I could tell he was proud of his Lakota Heritage, as he should be. His people had come through many hardships and had seen much pain.

Everyone including Spirit of Greywolf was now in the arena. "Let's Dance," he shouted.

My first presentation of the wolves would be in about a half hour, so as much as I wanted to stay in the arena area and watch the dancers, I knew I had to start walking back. I did make a mental note to make it back for the Men's Fancy Dance contest to watch Spirit of Greywolf and hope that he would be the winner of the purse.

When I got back to the wolves, there were already people waiting to see them. There was a lady very interested in one of my Black Hills Gold wolf pendants, so for now my mind was taken off Spirit of Greywolf. I knew it wouldn't be for long though!

20

This was the life for Spirit of Greywolf. He lived for the Pow Wows of his people. His mind wandered though to the red haired woman. Would this be the place he would meet the woman in his dreams? They were already into the women's jingle dance. Next would be the men's fancy dance, in which Spirit of Greywolf would be a participant. He was hoping he would win a portion of the purse. Someone tapped him on the shoulder.

"Ai, I can tell where your mind is. It is thinking of the wasicun winyan (white woman) you dream of. I believe you will meet her today. The nagi tanka (Great Spirit) will help you cinks (my son). You will bring her into the Lakota Oyate. You will make her your wife. Look to tatetob (the four winds) and to nagi tanka. I feel you will meet her, Spirit of Greywolf. You will make a life together and welcome little ones into your life. Your mother and father will be so happy you have found your soul mate. This woman of your dreams, you will live in the Paha Sapa (Black Hills). I feel this, Spirit of Greywolf. You are a good man and you will make this woman very happy. She will be your Wa-sna-win (storm woman) because she will whirl into your life. There is something I see, something in your name that has something connected to this woman, but I don't know exactly what it is. Don't worry, Spirit of Greywolf, she will be yours soon," Wild Running Horse said.

"Kola (friend), thank you. I believe you, for you can foresee the future. It has been proven many times. That is why I came to you to begin with. I knew you could help me," Spirit of Greywolf said.

"Hoppo (lets go) lets Pow Wow. It is time for the men's fancy dance!" Spirit of Greywolf exclaimed.

As he entered the circle with his number 1442 on his sleeve and his colorful costume with his wolf head, everyone clapped. Everyone had much respect for the wolf. Spirit of Greywolf gave it his all! He was a wonderful Lakota dancer. Everyone could tell he worked hard at what he did and that he was prouder than proud of his heritage. It was like he put his whole heart and soul into it. It was almost like his life depended on it. He danced around the arena as everyone watched his beautiful body with his rippling muscles and the color of bronze skin. He definitely was the best dancer in the arena. Everyone clapped and cheered for him.

21

Kiara couldn't tell which one was Spirit of Greywolf, because all the faces she could see were not his. There was one dancer though that had a wolf head on who seemed to be a favorite among the dancers. Could that possibly be him? She thought about his name, Spirit of Greywolf, and thought that it could be him. It would make sense, she thought. This was also one of the best Native American Dancers she had ever seen. It seemed as though he put his whole body and soul into his dance. She watched as his body moved about the arena, going up and down, touching the ground, and always coming up with his wolf head held proudly. It has to be him, she thought again. He would definitely be the winner of the purse tomorrow!

At every Pow Wow, the contestants competed for a prize of money. Today's first place dancer would win more money than Kiara had seen in the last six months, so that person would be very lucky. She watched that particular dancer for a long time. She knew it had to be him, because she couldn't take her eyes off of him. His colors danced around and around, up and down. Then she noticed the number, 1442, on his left armband. She somehow had to find out if it was indeed he. She watched him as she thought of all the Indian children she had met today. She had made arrangements to bring out her donations of toys and clothes to the reservation. There was a woman named Lori Rain Showers who she had met. She was the sweetest woman she had ever met. She had come up to her jewelry booth and was also at the wolf demonstration. She seemed especially fascinated with the wolves. They started talking and she was so easy to talk to that Kiara told her about the toys and clothes she had brought with her from Minnesota and that she wanted to donate them to the children on the Pine Ridge Reservation.

"That would be wonderful. A lot of us are very poor and would appreciate it very much. Of course, I don't have any little children. My son is a man now, but there are many other children that could use what you have. Please feel free to come by my house and we can go together and pass everything out and then you are welcome to come back to my house and eat my famous frybread. That's what my son says it is at least," Lori Rain Showers laughed.

It made Kiara realize how much these poor people needed things. She remembered the article she had read about how eighty percent of them were unemployed and the average family income was only $3,700 per year. How were they to live on this type of income? She also remembered reading about the high rate of alcoholism and thought to herself, how can you make someone quit something that makes them feel good and forget about the poor situation they live in? There was such a high suicidal rate among many of their teens because they felt that there is no future for them. Children are not supposed to feel like that. She thought of how, as a white woman, it was a disgrace what her race of people had done. If all she could do was help the children to a better way of life, to give them hope, she vowed she would! Not only would her wolves be her passion anymore, but these Indian children also would be. She would become friends with Lori Rain Showers and she would help her find a way to help the Lakota children to give them hope and a better future.

The closing of the Pow Wow for the day was over, so she walked back to her wolves to camp for the night. As she laid down, she also vowed she would meet this Spirit of Greywolf one day. Maybe there would be a time he could help her with this new passion she had found. She almost wished she could move to the reservation and help even more.

22

The next day was just as exciting as the last. Spirit of Greywolf did the best he could in the Men's Fancy Dance again. He hoped to be a winner of some of the prize money. He really hadn't had much time to walk around the Pow Wow grounds, since he had to stay close to the arena of dancers since he was the master of ceremonies. His mother, Lori Rain Showers, came to the arena to see him. She told him about the wonderful white woman she had met yesterday. She told him that she was there with her wolves and some of the most beautiful Black Hills Gold jewelry she had ever seen. She went on to tell him of how she had things she was going to bring to the reservation for the children. They had agreed she would come to Lori Rain Showers house on Tuesday.

"You should go meet her cinks, (my son)."

"I would so much like to go see her wolves, but I really need to stay here today until this is over. There is much to be done to close this Pow Wow tonight," Spirit of Greywolf said.

"I know cinks." She never even thought to tell him about the red hair on this white woman. She had never even thought that this was the woman her son had dreams about. She wondered now if maybe it was. "Spirit of Greywolf, would you be able to come to the house Tuesday when this woman named Kiara comes? Maybe we will need help with what she has. Maybe I could go see her again today and ask her if when she comes she could bring one or two of her wolves with her for you to see."

"Ai, Ina, I can do that for you. It would be nice if you can go see if she will bring her wolves with her too."

Just then, Spirit of Greywolf's Ate came up. "Spirit of Greywolf, you did wonderful in your dancing today. You are sure to win some of the purse," Chance Two Bears said.

"Ai. Pilamaya (thank you)," Spirit of Greywolf said to him.

"Come mitawin (my wife), let us go get some frybread and pejula sapa (coffee/) before they announce our son as the winner in the Mens Fancy Dance," he smiled.

Spirit of Greywolf's mother and father left and went up to the booth, because soon the winners would be announced.

Lori Rain Showers told her husband about the white woman with the wolves. She wanted to take him to meet her after they got their coffee and frybread, before the woman left, because she also wanted to ask her to bring one of her wolves on Tuesday to meet their son. When they got to Kiara's booth, she had many people buying her jewelry and three little children watching the wolves.

"Hello, this is my husband Chance Two Bears. I see you are very busy, so I won't keep you. I just wanted to ask you if you could bring one of your wolves with you on Tuesday? My son is here and I told him about you and your wolves. He would very much like to come over and see them, but he is very busy and can't get away, so I asked him if he could come help us on Tuesday and maybe you could bring one of your wolves to meet him. Do you think you can do this for me?" she smiled.

"Of course, it would be no problem. I will bring two other ones from home, so as to give these two a rest from this weekend and all the activity they had to go through these last two days," Kiara smiled back.

"Pilamaya (thank you). May the Nagi tanka bless you." Lori Rain Showers and her husband, Chance Two Bears, excused themselves so they could go see the winners of this year's Pow Wow and so Kiara could finish her sales and pack her wolves up to go home.

When they got to the arena, they were announcing the winner of the Men's Fancy Dance. "This year's winner of a portion of the purse for the Men's Fancy Dance is number 1442, Spirit of Greywolf!"

Spirit of Greywolf went up to the stage to collect his winnings while everyone clapped and cheered!

23

Kiara wished she could go see who the dance winners were, but she was just so busy she couldn't. Not that she was complaining, after all, this was how she made her living. She just wished she could have gotten just one more glimpse of this Spirit of Greywolf. This man that somehow over the past two days had mesmerized her.

She was packing her jewelry away. The wolves were a little restless, so she wanted to get on the road and get home so she could let them get back into their huge pen enclosure. She was sure they were anxious to see all their friends. She hated that they had been penned up for the last two days. She would wait until she got home to see how much she made, but she could tell she had done exceptionally well by how little she was putting away. She definitely would have to reorder before the next Pow Wow coming up in July at the Rosebud Casino. She didn't have anywhere to take the wolves next week, so they would have a week off. Except of course, when she went to see Lori Rain Showers on Tuesday. She would bring Shunkaha and Maheegan, but she also might bring two of the pups for the children to see.

Maybe Tacoma and Kayla. They were the two she was bringing to the library and nursing home next month, so this would be perfect timing for them.

It didn't take her long to get home. She was so happy when she pulled up to her house and saw Dr. Eagle out with the wolves.

"Well hello stranger," he said.

"Hi, how are my babies?" Kiara asked.

"They're doing wonderfully. Let me help you get these two back in the pen and you can all have a family reunion."

"Thanks," Kiara said.

They unloaded Chinook, Maheegan and Makala. As soon as they got them into the pen, all the other wolves started sniffing them and jumping all over them. Kiara had never seen such a wonderful and beautiful sight. She would be lost without these wonderful creatures God had created. God knew what he was doing when he created them, she thought, and she was so happy that he had put her into their life. After she gave them all treats and said good-bye to Dr. Eagle, she went in the house to have a bite to eat. She decided to unload her truck tomorrow and take inventory, since she had nothing else to do.

As she was eating her sandwich, she started thinking about going to the reservation on Tuesday. She wondered what Lori Rain Showers son looks like. She figured he liked wolves too, since he wanted her to bring one for him to meet. I hope I can create a bond with these children I am to meet, she thought. I would love to continue to help them as long as my means would allow me to. She remembered again about reading all the startling facts about the poor living conditions and unemployment on the reservation.

Kiara decided that she would give a portion of her money from the weekend to the new mothers, so they could buy milk for their babies. She wanted to do all she could to help and, even if she had to go without one meal for the week, it would be worth it. With that thought on her mind, she went to bed feeling really good and looking forward to Tuesday.

24

Although Spirit of Greywolf loved Pow Wows, he was happy to be home. He went to the corral to put Sunshine, Runs Like The Wind and Comes At Night back into their familiar surroundings. He loaded up the hay and water for them, locked the gate and started walking back to his tipi. He decided to put on a pot of coffee and sit by the fire for a while. He was still a little wound-up from the Pow Wow and decided to work on his paintings. He made a little extra money by selling these to a store down the road that featured work by local artists. As he painted a picture of the three horses, he daydreamed about the red headed woman. After what Wild Running Horse had told him before leaving for the Pow Wow, he thought for sure he would see her there, but he didn't. He was disappointed he did not find her yet. He was happy that he won a big chunk of the purse, though, and that his mother won a little something in the jingle dance. He decided he wanted to retire early tonight. He was tired and he knew that tomorrow he was going to finish some of his paintings and drop them at the store before he went to his mother's house. As he went into his tipi to lay down, he said a prayer.

"He-ay-hee-ee, nagi tanki let me dream again of this wasicun winyan (white woman), this wiwasteka, (beautiful woman) she is like a winyan wanagi (spirit woman). I want to meet her not only in my dreams, but also in my life. I need her in my life to make my journey here on earth complete. Please lead me to her. Lead me to this wiwasteka. With that last sentence, Spirit of Greywolf feel asleep.

His prayer was answered and he began to dream of the woman. They were at a Pow Wow, just like the one he had left. He had seen her from a distance. She was standing with a wolf by her side. She had her red hair in a braid down her back and she was looking up at the sky. He looked up to see what she was looking at, and saw it was an eagle. He was making dancing paths in the sky. He put his face down and looked back at her again. Just as he did this, she lowered her head and looked right into Spirit of Greywolf's eyes. She smiled and said something to her wolf and they both started walking towards him. When she got right across from him, she looked right into his eyes. Her eyes were the color of a clear blue pool. It started to lightly rain, so Spirit of Greywolf took off his shirt to shield her head from the raindrops. She looked down at his muscular chest with beads of rain falling on it. She reached her hand out and, with a gentle touch, rubbed it across his bottom lip. Then she put the whole palm of her hand on his chest to feel the strength he had there. His pectoral muscles were hard as a rock and she felt a stir within herself. Spirit of Greywolf lifted her chin.

"I have been looking for you. You are supposed to be in my life. I am drawn to you in life and in my dreams. Ohinyan, nimitawa kteto (forever you will be mine) wiwasteka. You will be my witamin (my wife). He reached down and ever so gently kissed her lips...

Spirit of Greywolf woke with a start. There were beads of

sweat forming all over his body. He was shaking. This dream was the most real dream he had ever had. He decided to walk down to the corral and check on his horses to clear his head. Although it was the middle of the night, he knew it would be hard for him to go back to sleep. He needed some cold air. Ai, he needed some cold air.

25

The Oglala Sioux Tribe had the second largest reservation in the United States. On the reservation was the Red Cloud Indian School, named after Chief Red Cloud. His burial site actually overlooked the school. Chief Bigfoot and Sitting Bull were also from this area. She wanted to go to Sitting Bulls grave sometime. She would like to put some flowers on it.

Kiara was having her morning coffee and reading some brochures she had picked up at the Pow Wow. She had already been out to the wolf pen and was going to get out her catalog to order more jewelry for the next Pow Wow. She went to get the boxes of jewelry she had left in her truck to take inventory. She had to finish packing the boxes for the children too. She had a big box of toys and books packed. She had another one with clothes and she wanted to make one up with food. She put the boxes on the floor and started unpacking them on the table. She poured herself another cup of coffee and started looking through the catalog to make out an order. She definitely would be ordering more wolf necklaces. She sold all sixteen of them at the last Pow Wow. Halfway through her work, she started daydreaming about the next day. She wondered what Lori Rain Showers son looked like and how his personality would be. She finished with her order and decided to put a cake in the oven before getting the children's food together. She thought it would be nice to bring this to Lori and her husband, Chance Two Bears. She started packing the box with cans of fruit and vegetables and a few cans of soup. She threw in a couple boxes of cereal and some oatmeal. She remembered the pens and pencils she had ordered to pass out to the school children at the library and went out and got some of them to pack too. With that all done, she went into the front room and lay on the couch to watch a wolf tape she had purchased awhile ago from The International Wolf Foundation that she never got a chance to watch.

26

Spirit of Greywolf was awake early since he couldn't really get back to sleep after his vivid dream. He would be going to his mother and father's today. He was excited to be able to meet a real wolf. The wolf was highly regarded in his nation. He wondered if this woman would allow him to interact with the wolf. He hoped so, of course, if it wasn't too dangerous

He decided to work on his paintings and give them a few finishing touches taking them to the store. The one he had started last night was one of his best paintings yet. He thought that he should bring his paints and a canvas with him today and paint one of this woman's wolves that he would meet. There was a slight chill in the air, but the sun was shimmering bright in the sky, so he knew it would warm up. He started a nice fire and got to work on his paintings. His mind wandered a little to the woman of his dreams again. If I ever do meet such a woman, he though, I will need to keep her close to me. I somehow feel she is destined to be with me. The spirits have shown me this. I will do whatever I can and whatever I have to so as to keep her in my life.

Soon, his paintings were all done and he went into his tipi to get ready to leave. This woman should have already made it to his mothers, so he didn't want to keep them. They would need his help, but he also knew his mother and there would be frybread and his father's coffee to eat and drink. Spirit of Greywolf laughed. Oh, but she was in for a treat, he thought. He put on some of the best clothes he had. He looked mighty handsome. He wondered why he was going through the trouble of looking his best when he didn't even know the woman. Maybe there was s a reason for it that had not yet been revealed. He packed three of his paintings in the truck and made it to the store within fifteen minutes. It wasn't far from where he lived or from the reservation.

"Hi Tokala," Spirit of Greywolf spoke.

"Hey Greywolf, its been awhile my friend. How have you been?" Tokala asked. Tokala and his wife, Running Waterfall, were the owners of the store.

"Fine, I just came back from the Pow Wow at the reservation."

"I suppose you won too?" Tokala smiled.

"Ai, I did."

"Good. I am glad you, for you are good at what you do, Spirit of Greywolf. In fact, I have some money for you here. I sold two of your paintings this month. You will need to bring me more." He handed an envelope to Spirit of Greywolf.

"I will. I painted one of horses last night, but I don't want to part with that one yet. I brought you these three today and I will bring you more before the next Pow Wow."

"That will be good. One of the women who bought a painting had bought one before. She said she liked your work. Especially the landscape of the Paha Sapa (Black Hills)."

"That is good I will do more."

This Paha Sapa he talked about was considered by the Lakota

Nation to be one of the oldest geological formations in the western hemisphere. They believed the hills were the basis of the Great Plains, where fresh water, vegetation and luck and beauty thrive. They have struggled for over 100 years to protect the land for future generations. As native people would say, "It is not the land that belongs to the people, it is the people that belong to the land."

Way back in 1858, the first non-natives entered this land. Ten years later, the Lakota Nation forced the United States to sign the Fort Laramie Treaty. The treaty guaranteed the greater part of five states to the Lakota Nation, in the center of which is Paha Sapa, Badlands and also the Lake Region where a lot of visitors come. One of the most famous places to visit is Mount Rushmore. The Great Sioux Nation had many things, such as the Wounded Knee Memorial Museum, Akta Lakota Museum and Cultural Center, and the Heritage Center at Red Cloud.

Visitors came from all over just to learn some of the Black Hills History. There really was so much to do here that you'd have to stay for weeks to do it all. The Animal Adventures was enough to bring tourists in. There was Black Country U.S.A., The Black Hills Wild Horse Sanctuary, Old McDonald's Farm, Reptile Gardens, Spirit of the Hills Sanctuary, The Roo Ranch, and D.C. Booth Historic National Fish Hatchery. There were also many theater productions, one of which was America's longest running stage productions, *The Black Hills Passion Play*.

"I must get going to my mother and fathers," Spirit of Greywolf said. "There is a white woman my mother met at the Pow Wow who is bringing clothing and food to the children on the reservation. She's also bringing a wolf. My mother says she raises them. I guess she brings them to the Pow Wows to educate the people about wolves. She also sells Black Hills Gold Jewelry."

"Go safe, Spirit of Greywolf. Don't forget that I expect more paintings from you. I can't sell what I don't have," Tokala said.

Spirit of Greywolf went out and got in his truck. He looked out over the Black Hills and thought how happy he was to be living in this place. He had been thinking that maybe tomorrow he would go to the Black Hills Caverns. He had not yet been there. It was a huge underground wind cavern. It had the Hills best variety of cave formations, including very rare logomites, helectities, stalactites, stalagmites, frost work and box work. 80% of the cave walls were lined with calcite crystals. He also had Bear Country U.S.A. and Reptile Ranch in mind to go see. He started his truck thinking he'd decide later and headed onto the reservation.

27

Kiara, Lori Rain Showers and her husband, Chance Two Bears, were sitting at the kitchen table eating frybread, drinking coffee and laughing. She had arrived at their house about a half hour ago and Lori Rain Showers had insisted she eat while waiting for Spirit of Greywolf.

"You are so kind, but you don't have to feed me," Kiara said.

"I know I don't have to. I want to. What you are doing for the children here is one of the kindest acts anyone could ever do. Here you are…new to the area of The Black Hills, your way of life, as you say, is simple, you have limited funds and yet even though you don't know my people, you are willing to give some of what you have to them. That shows much generosity. That shows a love deep in your soul for other humans that are less fortunate."

"My wife is right. You show much kindness to our people. Most are very poor here. Some say we should leave here and get a better way of life somewhere else, but what they don't understand is this is the only way of life we know. This is our heritage here. We don't want to leave and not be able to practice our ways. We are proud people. We value the earth greatly. Our ways may not be for all, but it is our ways. For your heart to go out to our children here is worth more than any amount of money in the world because you understand us. You are white, but you have a Lakota Trait. My wife admires you for that. I do too."

"Thank you," Kiara said with tears in her eyes.

They continued talking about the children and where they would go to bring the clothes, toys and food to be passed out. Kiara told them how she brought two of the pups for the children to see along with two full-grown wolves. Lori Rain Showers eyes sparkled.

"They will be so excited. I am so glad I stopped at your booth and met you. You are a wonderful woman to open your heart to our people," she smiled with tears in her eyes.

Just then, there was a knock at the door. The door opened and Kiara saw the man from the Pow Wow. She couldn't believe her eyes. This was Lori Rain Showers son? His frame seemed to fill the whole door. His body was so muscular. His skin was a glistening bronze color. She couldn't take her eyes off of him.

Spirit of Greywolf stood in the doorway frozen! He couldn't even shut the door. He was looking into the eyes of the woman of his dreams! Her blue eyes and that red hair...it was she. He knew it in his heart. She was exactly as he had pictured her. Is this the woman his mother met? It had to be, otherwise why would she be here?

"Spirit of Greywolf, shut the door," Lori Rain Showers scolded. "What is wrong with you? You look as if you have seen a ghost."

"Nothing, I am fine," he said not taking his eyes off of Kiara.

"Well Kiara, this is my *cinks*, which means son in our language," Lori Rain Showers said. "Spirit of Greywolf, this is the woman I told you about from the Pow Wow. Her name is Kiara."

"Hello K-I-A-R-A," he said her name very slowly as if trying to etch it in his mind.

"Hello," was all Kiara could get out.

"Sit cinks, have some frybread and coffee before we go. Kiara has also brought two of her wolf pups and two of her full grown wolves for the children and for you to see," his mother said.

Spirit of Greywolf sat down right next to Kiara. Neither could take their eyes off the other. Chance Two Bears noticed this. Then it dawned on him that this woman must be the one his son has been dreaming about. The one he has talked about for months. This had to be her. She looked exactly the way he described.

"I am sorry to stare at you, but you are so beautiful and I feel as if I have met you somewhere before. Like I know you from another time," Spirit of Greywolf said.

"That's ok. I feel as if I also know you from somewhere also. We never officially met, but I saw you opening day of the Pow Wow. I sell Black Hills Jewelry and I educate people about wolves. I'm sure I would have remembered if I had met you." She felt herself blush, so she quickly continued, "I moved here not long ago from Minnesota and I just started doing Pow Wows this way this year. I always went out west before, like to Arizona and New Mexico. The Black Hills really caught my eye, though, when I visited here so I packed up my wolves and moved right after that. This is what I do for a living, so it really doesn't matter where I live," she felt her face growing hot.

"No, I never met you in a physical sense, but I feel I have met you in a spirit world. I know I have," Spirit of Greywolf just couldn't take his eyes off of her.

Kiara smiled.

"Eat cinks," his mother said.

Spirit of Greywolf picked up his frybread and took a bite,

never taking his eyes off of Kiara. She also didn't take her eyes off of him. His parents noticed this and his father reached over and squeezed Lori Rain Showers hand and smiled. They both knew this was the woman of their son's dreams. They both knew he would make her his wife. She would soon be in their family and they couldn't think of anyone that would be better for their son. They both smiled because they had never seen their son look so happy. He only had eyes for this woman. It was almost like they weren't even in the room with him.

After some time, Lori said they should get going because the children would be waiting for them.

"We should be able to fit in my truck," Kiara said.

So they all went outside and got in her truck. Spirit of Greywolf was in the passenger seat, as comfortable as he had been there for years. They pulled up in front of a building where there were children playing stick ball. When they saw Lori Rain Showers, they all came running to give her hugs and kisses and all started talking at once.

"I will take these boxes you have and bring them in the building. I do not want you bringing these in by yourself," Spirit of Greywolf said.

"It is no trouble at all. I enjoy doing nice things for someone who is less fortunate than I am," Kiara said.

"Well ok, but you carry the light ones and let me carry the heavy ones," Spirit of Greywolf said with a wink.

They brought the boxes into the building and Lori Rain Showers explained that she was going to pass everything out while Kiara brought the wolves in. Kiara went outside to start getting her wolves ready to bring in, with Spirit of Greywolf right behind her. He hadn't taken his eyes off of her once since seeing her at his mother's table.

"Can I help?" he asked.

"Sure you can get the pups." She took him to the back of the truck and opened the latch. "This is Kayla and this is Tacoma. I named him after my truck," she laughed.

"Oh, they are adorable," Spirit of Greywolf was laughing, as they pulled at his clothes.

"Back here we have Shunkaha, who is a male. His name means "wolf," but I'm sure you already know that. This is Maheegan."

"Ai, I do speak and understand the language," Spirit of Greywolf told her.

They brought the wolves in and Kiara gave her presentation. She stayed there for three hours, which was the longest she had ever stayed anywhere with the wolves. She just didn't want to leave. She felt so at home with these people and comfortable with the children and with this new family she had met. She glanced over at Spirit of Greywolf, only to see him staring at her. He smiled and so did she. She felt a stirring in her chest she had never felt before. She could have sworn that he winked at her, but she could be wrong. He got up and walked over to where she was sitting.

"I haven't been able to take my eyes off of you, you are a wiwasteka. In Lakota, that means beautiful woman. Your hair is like fire and your eyes are like pools of the bluest of blue water. I do not want you to leave me. I don't have much, K-I-A-R-A. I am a very simple man with a very simple life. I live right outside of this reservation in a tipi, just like my people did many years ago. It is huge though and it is beautiful just like you. I believe you would like it. I do all my own cooking outside. I own three horses. Actually, my Sunshine and Runs Like the Wind just had a colt that I named Comes At Night. Come stay the night with me. I will explain to you why I was looking at you so strangely since I first saw you at my mothers table."

"I want to say yes to you. Its almost like I am under some kind of spell, but I can't. I have my wolves to tend to. Not only do I have these, but also I have five more pups and six more that are full grown ones. I couldn't just leave them alone and these four need to go back home," Kiara said sadly.

"I understand. How about tomorrow? Will you spend the day with me? I have some places in mind I'd like to go to, but also since you sell Black Hills Gold, I know of a special place to take you to. I'm sure since you just moved out here you've never been to The Mt. Rushmore Gold Factory and Outlet Store have you?" he asked.

"No I haven't," she replied.

"Well they have a guided Diamond and Black Hills Gold Jewelry Tour that I'm sure you would enjoy and I would love to take you. Then I would love to take you to a cavern or to Bear's U.S.A. I believe they have wolves there…or we can go anywhere else you want to. Just so I can spend the day with you…please say yes K-I-A-R-A," he almost sounded as if he was going to cry.

"I would love to go with you and anywhere would be fine with me," she smiled.

"Great, give me directions to your house and I will help you get the wolves back into your truck."

He helped her load the wolves into the back of the truck and told her he would be at her house at ten o'clock in the morning. She thanked his mother and father. Lori Rain Showers told her the children had never been so excited. They all waved as Kiara left. Spirit of Greywolf wished he was going with her, but tomorrow would have to be soon enough. He hugged his mother and father goodbye and told them about tomorrow. They just smiled at him because they knew what was in their son's head. They knew Kiara would be their daughter-in-law soon.

28

Spirit of Greywolf was up early. He didn't sleep very well, although he did not have the dream. He couldn't sleep because he was so excited about today. He laid in his tipi thinking about meeting Kiara that day. He knew as soon as he saw her sitting at his mother's table that she was the woman of his dreams. He was extremely happy and very much at ease. He thought about how he would tell her about his dreams that he believed she was the woman he was dreaming about. He didn't want to scare her off though. He hardly even knew this woman, but he did know one thing. She was the woman he would grow old with and spend the rest of his life with. They were meant to be together.

He drank his coffee and thought about where they would go today. He thought about what he should wear. He wanted to look his best for her. He wanted her to want him as much as he wanted her. I wonder what her house looks like, he thought. I hope she will also show me the rest of her wolves! Will she let me stay the night with her tonight or will I have to wait until I make her my wife? I could make her my wife right away. Today if she would let me.

TINA VELAZQUEZ

Spirit of Greywolf had never even thought about getting married. He was very satisfied with the way his life was, but with the dreams of this woman and now meeting Kiara, he knew she was the woman from his dreams. He knew he had to marry her. He wanted her for the rest of his days on this earth. He would be with this wiwasteka.

He thought about this marriage and he would ask her if it was okay to have a Native American Wedding custom called the Blanket Ceremony. Both the bride and the groom were given a blue blanket, which represented all of the sorrows and hardships in their past lives. They are wrapped in these blankets at the beginning of the ceremony, then after the blessing of the union, the blue blankets are removed and the couple is wrapped in one white blanket together which they wear for the remainder of the ceremony. They are then one together and no longer separate. He wanted to marry this woman right away. He didn't want to even wait one day! He would ask her today if he could get up the nerve. At that thought, he left to go and get her. He couldn't wait to see her again.

When he pulled up in front of her house, she was sitting on the front porch in a rocking chair. What a vision she was to him! Only this time she wasn't a dream. She was real and he was going to make her his wife. He got out of his truck. "Hello K-I-A-R-A," he said.

"Hello to you," she smiled. She watched as he walked from his truck up to her porch. He had a way about him that made him very attractive to her. He had his hair in a long braid down his back and the sun shining behind him with his glistening muscles made her think of things she had never thought of before. He had on a t-shirt that, at this very moment, she thought she'd like to rip off of him. "Well, where shall we go first? I have a busy day planned for us and I believe at the end of it you will be shocked at what I am going to ask you," he said.

"You mean you're going to make me wait all day in suspense as to what the question is?" she smiled.

With that smile his heart just melted. "Ai, you must wait. I believe we will go to The Mt. Rushmore Gold Factory and Outlet Store last because there is something there I need to purchase," he responded.

Kiara looked at him puzzled. What would he be purchasing that had to be bought at the end of the day?

"We should go to the Cavern first, then to Bears U.S.A. After that, we can go to lunch and onto your Black Hills Gold store where I truly believe you will get something very special," he winked at her.

"Sounds good to me. I am looking forward to spending the day with you, Spirit of Greywolf." She couldn't tell him that she was so excited last night about spending the day with him today that she couldn't sleep. All she kept thinking of was when she first saw him at the Pow Wow and then at his mothers. His voice sounded so sexy, especially when he said her name. He always pronounced it very slowly. Then she was impressed by how good he was with the children. She wondered if he had ever been married or if he had any children of his own. He seemed like he'd be a really good dad, not to mention husband. "Do you want to go see my other wolves and the rest of the pups first before we leave? Or would you like to wait until we get back?" she asked.

"How about when we get back? I believe we might want to sit and talk awhile when this day is over and what a better place than right here," he smiled.

"All right then...let's go," Kiara said.

Spirit of Greywolf opened the door of his truck and Kiara got in. She noticed he had a small blue and red dream catcher hanging from his mirror. It had a small wolf in the middle of it. He got in the truck and started the engine. She couldn't take her eyes off of him. She couldn't help but look at him and smile. He was so handsome. He had a very straight nose and his lips looked so kissable...it took all of her strength to not just reach out and put her lips on his. She had never had thoughts about anyone as she did with this man! But then again, she had never met anyone like him that turned her head in circles and made her heart do flips.

They had just gone past Mt. Rushmore. She could see where they were still working on carving out Crazy Horse. Of course, there were the presidents, Washington, Jefferson, Lincoln and Theodore Roosevelt. She could see all of them very well from the road.

"I wonder if Crazy Horse will ever get done," she asked.

Ai, someday hopefully. It would be nice to see it done. This is such beautiful land. I've lived here all of my life. I grew up on the Pine Ridge Reservation and when I got older, I moved to right outside of there. I have a passion for this land. You must come and see my tipi and horses K-I-A-R-A," Spirit of Greywolf said.

She loved the way he said her name. It made her tingle all over. At that moment, even though she didn't know him well, there was something about him that she thought she'd do anything for him. She didn't think she'd ever be able to say no to him!

"I'm sure I will. I would love to meet your horses, especially your new pony. I'd love to see where you live too."

"This will be a nice drive. I hope you will enjoy your day with me K-I-A-R-A," he said.

"I'm sure I will. I am already. I can't wait to go to this Black Hills Gold Store you told me about," she said.

"Me neither. I want very much to get something there. I believe today could change both of our lives forever. Tell me...why did you move here?" he asked.

"Well, I've always been fascinated with the Lakota culture. But my love of wolves and the beauty of the land just made me realize it was time for a change in my life. I was at a job that I hated. I used to go to any Pow Wows I could find. The colors of the costumes, the dancers, the food and the music...everything about them made me feel alive. I got through my week just thinking about the next Pow Wow I could go to. They took me away from the real world one I couldn't even see myself living in anymore.

When I'd go to the Pow Wows, I felt like I was in a different world...a world where everything was beautiful. One day I woke up and decided I needed a major change in my life. So when I was here at a Pow Wow, I got a newspaper and I saw a house for sale. I decided to go look at it and when I did, I saw all I could do with it. It wasn't in the best shape, but I could afford it and it had a lot of land for my wolves. Little by little I'm doing things to improve it. Anyway, I went home and packed up my things and left just like that! No regrets!

Then I had to decide how I was going to make money out here, so I took my two greatest passions in life, wolves and Native American history, and started going to Pow Wows and educating people about wolves. I had a Black Hills Gold necklace of a wolf and thought that maybe I could sell this kind of jewelry. I checked into it and got in contact with a wholesaler and started doing that. Now, I also bring my wolves to the library and show them to children and recently I started going to a nursing home out here," she took a breath.

"That is wonderful. I am very proud to have met you and I hope you will get to know me. I feel a great connection to you K-I-A-R-A. Maybe I was meant to meet you. You have this love of wolves...and my name is Greywolf. It is like an omen of some kind. Then, well there is another reason that maybe one day I could tell you about," he smiled.

"I feel connected to you too. Maybe it does have to do with

your name and my love of wolves, or maybe because of your heritage and my passion for it," she smiled too.
   They kept driving and he reached over and took her hand. Kiara's stomach did somersaults. Her heart beat faster and there was a stirring deep down within her body. It was like butterflies were flying around. For some reason, she squeezed his hand. Maybe to make sure this was really happening. It felt so normal to hold his hand. It felt so right…like she had been doing this all her life.
   They got to The Black Hills Cavern and Spirit of Greywolf paid for them to go in. What a crystal show cave it was! They signed up for the Adventure Tour, which was sixty minutes long covering three levels of the cave. It was amazing how much was underground that most people didn't know about. When they came out of the cave, they went into the gift shop. Spirit of Greywolf bought Kiara a crystal stone.
   "Here it matches the blue of your eyes," he said.
   "Thank you," she smiled again.
   He held the door open for her again and she got in the truck. "Well now onto Bear Country U.S.A.," he said.
   This was an exciting and unique drive thru a wildlife park with bears, wolves, elk, and twenty-five different animals on over two hundred acres of Black Hills scenic beauty. After the three-mile drive, they enjoyed a leisurely walk through "baby land" that had the babies and other small residents.
   "They have a restaurant here called Hungry Bear Café. Do you want to eat before we go to our last stop? Then we'll go to the gift shop so I could buy you a wolf statue," Spirit of Greywolf said.
   "Yes, that would be fine, but you don't have to buy me a statue! You already bought me something today," Kiara said.
   "Ai, I do…and wait until you see what I buy on our last stop wiwasteka," he said. Now it was Spirit of Greywolfs turn to smile.

They ate and went in the gift shop where he bought her a statue of a mother and father wolf with their pups. "I know it's not five but it'll have to do," he said.

"Thank you again," Kiara smiled.

They got back in the truck and he opened the door again for her. What a gentleman, she thought. He immediately took her hand this time when he got in after putting the truck in drive.

On the drive to the Black Hills Gold Factory and Outlet store in Rapid City, Kiara asked Spirit of Greywolf if he had ever heard of the Black Hills Wild Horse Sanctuary? She had seen it advertised in a book she had been looking at.

"Ai, it is in Hot Springs. Why do you ask?" he said.

"Well, I just thought maybe we could go there together someday, since you have horses. It would be nice for you to see what you raise," she said.

"We will have many days together K-I-A-R-A and yes I would love to go there with you. I want to bring you riding with me one day too. You can ride Sunshine, but I want to wait a little while since it hasn't been that long ago since she gave birth."

"Oh, I would love that!" she exclaimed.

When they got to the store, they took the guided Diamond and Black Hills Gold tour. Kiara loved every minute of it. Since she sold this jewelry, it was great to see how it was made. What really surprised her was when Spirit of Greywolf brought her over to a goldsmith who did custom jewelry design. He looked over at the man, and the man smiled. It was almost like they had talked before. Kiara watched as Spirit of Greywolf held her hand and got down on one knee. She looked at him.

"K-I-A-R-A, I know I have just met you, but you have been in my life longer than you know. You have been in my dreams every night and now I have met you and I know you are the woman I want to spend the rest of my life with. Please tell me you will be my mitawin, my wife. I will make you the happiest woman in the world and we will create our own world together. There is nothing we will not be able to conquer together. You are my wiwasteka, my beautiful woman. I need to have you to share the rest of my life in this world and beyond through eternity. Please K-I-A-R-A, tell me yes," Spirit of Greywolf said. He had tears in his eyes and running down his cheeks.

Kiara looked at him, tears forming in her own eyes. She didn't even really know this man. She had just met him, but she felt like she had known him forever. Forever, since she went to the first Pow Wow she had searched for him. For a Lakota man to love. This was her destiny. She loved wolves and his name said wolf. She remembered the day of the Pow Wow when she first saw him, and she thought she fell in love with him then. She looked at him with tears in her eyes and said,"...YES! I feel like I have waited my whole life for you too!"

"K-I-A-R-A, my wiwasteka, my witawin," Spirit of Greywolf cried.

He stood up and picked her up. He twirled her around and shouted to everyone in the store that she said yes. She was going to be his wife. They would be together forever and through all eternity. He was crying. She was crying. The store clerk had tears in his eyes and everyone else was clapping and cheering. He looked at the man who did the custom jewelry design. "I told you she'd say yes. She had to."

Kiara looked at him as he hugged her and playfully slapped his hard muscled chest.

"Now I need you to make up two wedding bands with wolves running around them for our wedding." He looked at Kiara. "Is that okay with you? I know your love of wolves, but if that is not what you want we can change it."

"No, it's perfect, she said."

"Now I want her to have whatever kind of diamond ring she wants for the engagement ring. Nothing is to good for my K-I-A-R-A."

The man took her over to a case with diamond engagement rings in it. She picked out a ring with a small heart shaped diamond with two blue sapphires on each side.

"Is this okay, Spirit of Greywolf?" she asked.

"Anything you want is okay with me. I just want to marry you. I don't want to wait. I need these rings today," he told the man. "This week, within a few days, we will marry. K-I-A-R-A you will be my mitawin."

He kissed her gently and she kissed him back. This was like a dream to her. Someone slap me and wake me up, she thought. I can't believe this is really happening. But it was, she realized this as the store clerk was sizing her finger for her rings and Spirit of Greywolf for his. He paid another clerk for his purchase all the time with only eyes for her!

29

As they drove home, the ring sparkled on her finger. Kiara felt like she was on a cloud. Spirit of Greywolf had a permanent smile on his face. He squeezed her hand tightly and told her how much he loved her. She in turn told him the same.

"K-I-A-R-A, I want to marry you right away. This week as soon as we can. Is that all right with you? I don't want to spend another sleepless night without you. Stay with me tonight K-I-A-R-A."

"I have to stay where my wolves are, Spirit of Greywolf. I've been gone all day."

"Can I stay by you then? I can leave my horses until tomorrow. They will be fine. I want to talk about our wedding. Tomorrow we will have to go tell my mother and father. They will be happy for both of us. They really like you."

"What did you mean back in the store when you said I had been in your dreams?" Kiara asked.

Spirit of Greywolf looked over at her and said, "For months I have been having these reoccurring dreams of a red-haired woman with blue eyes. As soon as I saw you at my mother's table,

LAKOTA DREAMS

I knew that woman was you. This woman in my dreams has been a vision to me and when I saw you, I knew I had to make you my wife. I had to make you mine. You were the woman who came to me every night. We were meant to journey this world together. This woman is you K-I-A-R-A. Every time I look at you my heart flutters. My dreams have come true. You have finally come into my life. You have come out of my dreams and into my life. I will never make you regret marrying me so quickly. I will treat you like the delicate flower that you are. My Lakota name for you will be Dream Come True, because that is what you are to me, a dream that has come true. Now please tell me I can stay with you tonight. I will sleep on your floor, I promise. We have so much to talk about. We have to make plans for our wedding. Please say yes," he said, pouting his lips.

Looking into his eyes and then at the beautiful diamond on her finger, how could she say no? "Okay, but you will sleep on the couch next to the fire. It will keep you warm through the night. That is the only hotness you will get," she laughed.

"I promise I will not do anything you don't want me to do before our wedding. I just need to know you are near me," he said.

They continued to drive until the sun was setting. When they pulled up to her house, she got out of the truck and told Spirit of Greywolf she needed to go check on the pups.

"Ai, I want to see them too. May I?" he asked.

"Of course, they now will be part of your life too. As will be your horses be part of mine," she said.

"Ai, they will. Everything that is mine is now yours too K-I-A-R-A. Just promise me that from tonight on you, will be mine forever and that every night when the sun leaves the sky you will be in my arms," Spirit of Greywolf asked with tears in his eyes.

"I will. For some reason, I feel like you were sent to me. The Pow Wow circuit changed my life years ago and I knew that you are what I was looking for. From the moment I saw you and heard your name, I knew you were the one for me. Then meeting your mother…what was the chance of that? And what was the chance that you would be her son? You're right…somehow we were both brought together for some reason beyond our control. We were brought into each others lives and I promise to love you for life," she squeezed his hand.

He tilted her head back with his hands and kissed her gently.

"Techihhila K-I-A-R-A. That means *I Love You*.

"Techihhila, Spirit of Greywolf. I hope you can teach me more of your language over the years," she said.

"I will. I am a good teacher. Now let us go see your wolves. He took her hand and they walked over to the huge enclosure. She introduced him to everyone, even the pups. They all started howling and Spirit of Greywolf howled with them and started laughing. He tried to howl louder than them and that made Kiara start laughing. After doing this for about twenty minutes, they walked to the house. As they walked in the door, Spirit of Greywolf felt very much at home. Kiara had pictures and statues of Native Americans throughout her house. She really did follow the history people. He even saw a medicine wheel on the wall. Kiara watched him as he looked around.

"It needs a little work yet, but it's comfortable to me," she said.

"It is beautiful just like you. There is nothing wrong with it that I can see," Spirit of Greywolf said.

"Let me make us some coffee. Please sit and make yourself comfortable. I will get you a pillow and blanket. I have some apple pie for our coffee too. Would you like some?" she asked.

"Ai, thank you. I will go out and get your gifts from the truck while your doing that. I see a table over there where they can find a home," he smiled.

Kiara went into the kitchen to get the pie and coffee. As she waited for the coffee to get done, she went into the bedroom and got the pillow and blanket and brought them into the front room. When she got the, Spirit of Greywolf was putting the statue on the table.

"I have something else for you K-I-A-R-A. He reached into his pocket and gave her a little box. It was from the Black Hills Gold store where they got their rings.

"What is this? You bought me enough today," she said.

"You are my woman to spoil. Just open it," he said.

She opened the box and saw that it was a necklace with a wolf howling. It was of Black Hills Gold and it was beautiful. "Oh Spirit of Greywolf, it's beautiful! I love it. I love you. Thank you so much." She had tears in her eyes. She couldn't believe what her life had given her over the last few days. She had never been so happy.

"Le mita pila, *my thanks* and you are hohahe that means, *welcome*. Turn around and let me help you put it on," he said.

He put the necklace on her and turned her around to face him. He kissed her gently. They looked into each other's eyes and smiled. Neither could believe their good fortune.

"My Dream Come True, that is you," he smiled.

"Let me start a fire. There is a chill in the room," Spirit of Greywolf said.

"Ai and I will get the coffee," Kiara said.

"Coffee, *pejula sapa*, which also means black medicine," he told her.

"I will never be able to remember all these words, but I will try," she laughed. She came out of the kitchen with the pie and coffee into a nice warm fire lit room. They watched the fire and talked about going to his mother and father's tomorrow and telling them the good news.

"Thank you for today. I sure never thought when I left this

morning that my life was going to change forever by this evening," Kiara said.

"Ai it will, but I promise to always make you happy. You better go and get some sleep now. We have much to talk about in the morning before going to my mother's," Spirit of Greywolf smiled.

Kiara wished him good night and gave him a kiss. She went into the bedroom and got ready for bed. She laid in bed thinking about the events of today and still couldn't believe how it had turned out. She was so happy though. It was like she had been waiting her entire life for this day to happy. She also would make him happy. How could she not? She went to sleep with a smile on her face.

30

When she awoke the next morning, Spirit of Greywolf was already in the kitchen. "Good morning. I have made you some coffee and frybread. I take it you slept well?" he asked.

"Yes, I guess the events of the day really wore me out," she responded.

"Sit and have something to eat and we will talk about our future together." He pulled out a chair for her and brought her some of the frybread and a cup of coffee. He started talking to her about their wedding. He wanted to marry her as soon as possible, if that was okay with her. He had some ideas. They could go get married in this little chapel called Chapel In The Hills. Or they could just get married on the reservation by one of his people. They could have a blanket ceremony. He went on to tell her what that consisted of.

"I would like very that very much. It would be different and it would take place where you grew up. What about where we will live? I have to have a place for my wolves if we don't stay here," Kiara said.

"Ai, I had thought about this last night and I will tell you what

I think and you tell me if it is acceptable to you. If no and you would want something else, tell me…because it is up to you where we live. What if because you have so much land we could stay here in this house on cold winter nights and I could move my tipi on some part of the back land and we could stay in there in the summer? Your wolves would stay where they are used to and I could build a corral for the horses further back away from the wolves. That way we could be one big happy family," Spirit of Greywolf said.

"That is a wonderful idea. Did you stay up all night figuring that out? We will also keep doing what we do for a living by going to the Pow Wows right?" she asked.

"Of course, but with both of us and only one place to live it will also be cheaper. We are going to have a wonderful life together K-I-A-R-A. I promise you this. Let us go feed your wolves now. We need to go check on my horses before going to the reservation. Maybe we can go riding today, Ai?" he asked.

"That would be nice," she said.

They went out and fed the wolves and then drove to his place where he introduced her to his horses. He took her to his tipi to show her where he lived. It was beautiful and really roomy. She couldn't believe it. The whole inside was Native American décor. He had dream catchers all around his bed. She even noticed before she went in that he had horses and a wolf painted on the outside hide. He had a fire with huge stones in the middle. He lit some sweet grass in a bowl next to the fire.

"Please sit for awhile before we leave. I want you to have the feel of the inside. I want you to become part of my world today."

She sat down and asked him if it would be hard for him to move the tipi.

"No, it is very easy actually to take down and just as easy to put back up, but first thing tomorrow I will start to build the new corral for our horses. It will only take me a few days. Then I will move the tipi. That will be done in one day. In the meantime though, you will let me stay on your couch, ai? I don't ever want to be apart from you. Not even for a minute. We will wait until we are married to share your bed. I will respect that much," he smiled at her.

"Yes, all that is fine with me." It was her turn to smile.

"Good. Let us go now to my mother and father's. We will talk to the man that will marry us and see if three days from now is okay."

They left and went to his mother and father's. Lori Rain Showers was not surprised to see them come through the door. She could tell yesterday that there was a connection between the two of them. When Spirit of Greywolf told her they were to be married, she smiled and put her hands to her mouth.

"I knew she was the one for you! I am so happy for you both." She came and hugged Kiara and then her son.

"Hohahe. I am so happy you two have found each other."

His father got up from the table and shook his son's hand and also welcomed Kiara into their family.

"When will you be married," his mother asked?

"We are going to talk to Black Elk to see when he can have a blanket ceremony for us. It is what we have decided on. Hopefully within a few days. I will be moving my tipi to Kiara's land and building a corral within the next few days."

"Oh! I need to start preparing. I have a celebration to get ready for. There is so much to do." His mother was running around the kitchen as if it was her wedding to prepare for. You wouldn't have been able to get the smile off of her face if you tried.

They left to go talk to Black Elk, who agreed to marry them in three days on the reservation. Then they went back to Spirit of Greywolf's and took the horses out for a ride. They both rode bareback. When they came back, Spirit of Greywolf loaded his truck with boards to take back to Kiara's to start building his corral. He had never been so happy.

31

The next day, Spirit of Greywolf started working on the corral for the horses. He wanted to work on it all day so he would be able to move his horses here and start on moving his tipi. He wanted to get everything done within the next few days, because on the third day would be their wedding. He had never been so happy in his entire life. Just to think…this all came about because of his dreams. He really did believe that Wanka Tanka was responsible for bringing Kiara into his life.

Kiara came out to where he was working on the corral with a cup of coffee for him. "Hey it looks like it's coming along," she said.

"Ai, I will work all day to get it done, so it will only take me one day instead of the two I thought. Then tomorrow you will be able to help me start packing up the tipi to move before our wedding day, ai?" he asked.

"Yes, I will be able to. But right now I'm taking Denali and the pups to the library. It is their day. Then I have a one-hour presentation at the nursing home. I'm only supposed to go there once a month, but I wanted everyone to see the pups while they're still small. I won't be late though. There's food in the house if you get hungry."

"I'll be fine out here. I want to make sure I get this all done. When you come home we'll eat. Then we'll go get Sunshine, Runs Like the Wind, and Comes At Night. I'm sure they'll love it here. We will be one big happy family in a few days," he smiled.

Spirit of Greywolf took her in his arms and kissed her deeply while telling her how much he loved her. She then went to load up her truck with Denali, Casey, Kayla, and Cailin. She decided to take the last two pups, Misun and Tacoma. Boy, what a load I have today, she thought.

She got to the library and Dana was there to help her as always.

"Hi how've you been? How was the nursing home after here last time? What about the Pow Wow?" she asked.

"Hey one question at a time!" she laughed. "But if I told you about the Pow Wow and what happened after, you'd never believe it."

"Why? What happened? Just answer that question!" Dana begged.

Kiara went on to tell her about the residents for the nursing home first. She told her they just loved the wolves. She told her about how she even went over her time. That she just couldn't leave with the smiles on their faces. Then came the shocker. She told her about the Pow Wow and meeting Lori Rain Showers, about Spirit of Greywolf, their outing and his proposal.

"You're what? Getting married in three days!" she exclaimed"

"Ai, which means yes in the Lakota language that I am also learning. I will be getting married in three days! On the Pine Ridge Reservation, in what is called a Blanket Ceremony. We will live in my house, but he is bringing his tipi to put up by the house and today he is building a corral for his horses. Will you come and see us get married? I would really like that," Kiara said.

"Of course, just call me with the time. I think that would be awesome to go to a Native American Wedding Ceremony!" Dana exclaimed.

"Okay, I will let you know! Now let's get these guys out of their cages," Kiara said.

They brought the all the wolf puppies in a few cages. Then Kiara went and got Denali on a leash. These children had already heard the long speech about wolves. They were back so soon just to see the pups that had been born. Of course, she had to bring their mama Denali with too.

The children were so excited to see the pups. They even got to feed them some bottled milk and play with them on the floor for a while. Some of the children asked if they could take one home. Of course, Kiara explained how you had to have a special license to have them and lots of room and pens that were really safe for both them and humans. The children wanted to know if she'd bring them back again.

When it was time to go, Kiara told Dana she'd call her tomorrow about the time. Then she remembered they had already set the time! Three o'clock. She went on to tell her to come to her house at two and that way she'd get to meet Spirit of Greywolf and just follow them to the reservation.

"Okay, I'll be there at two," Dana said.

When Kiara got to the nursing home, the residents were already in the room waiting for her. They were so excited about meeting the pups that they just couldn't wait! You would have thought they were as excited as the children. Ann came out to help Kiara. They did the same as at the library getting all the wolves out. When they saw the pups, they all wanted to hold one. Their eyes were aglow. It was a beautiful sight to see all the smiles on their faces.

Kiara gave a bottle each to five of the residents. She told them they had just eaten at the library, but they could try. Well of course, the pups ate like they hadn't been fed in months! The residents were laughing and having a great time. Kiara smiled and knew she'd be here longer than an hour. How could she leave when they were all so happy?

She had been right too! Two hours later, she was loading them back into the truck and the people in the nursing home didn't want them to go even then. They would have kept them all night if she would have let them.

By the time she got home it was close to five o'clock. Spirit of Greywolf saw her pull up and came running out to help her unload the wolves...but not before giving her a kiss.

"I missed you something awful! I couldn't wait for you to get back. I worked non-stop though and the corral is all finished, so we can go and get the horses. After you have something to eat though," Spirit of Greywolf said.

They put all the wolves back in their pen. All the other wolves came running up to greet them. Dakota checked out each one of the pups to make sure they were okay. Next time I'll have to bring him to show everyone the dad, she thought. Denali was tired and went to lie down by the tree after she had something to eat and some water.

We went in the house and I started to make us some hamburgers and fries while Spirit of Greywolf went to take a shower.

When he came back out into the kitchen, he smelled wonderful. He looked wonderful! He hadn't braided his hair yet and it was all wet and straight halfway down his back. I wondered how I ever got so lucky to meet this man. The scent of his soap was driving me crazy. I put our plates on the table and walked over to him. I put my arms around him and kissed his lips. They were moist and warm. He in turn put his arms around my waist and told me again how much he had missed me and how much he loved me.

"I am so glad I have met you. I do love you and I promise we will have a very happy life together," Kiara said.

"I too love you K-I-A-R-A, more than you can ever imagine. I never want to be parted from you. You are my other half now. Without you I am not whole. I have searched my dreams for you and now here you are all mine," he smiled at her.

He kissed her again while rubbing her arms and her back. She kissed him back with an urgency she never knew she had. She ran her fingers through his long hair and pressed her body into his. She heard him moan her name softly. Then he was talking in his native tongue. She heard him say my *wiwasteka, my mitawin*. A smile came over her face. Their kisses became more passionate and more urgent. He was kissing her eyes, nose, cheeks and forehead. His hands rubbed her body. She was squeezing his muscles on his arms and rubbing the back of his neck. Then all of a sudden he pulled her away to arms length.

"I am sorry, but as you can see I am getting very aroused by you and I made a promise to you. We only have two days until we become husband and wife. Then I will be able to make love to you in the only way a man can love a woman so fully. But it can only be when you are my wife. That is the way Wanka Tanka says."

"I know, I understand. I don't know what came over me. You're just so wonderful to me and so handsome. I lost my mind for a minute, but your right we do need to wait until the time is right," Kiara said. She picked up their plates and laughed saying, "Thank God for microwaves."

Spirit of Greywolf laughed too as he was jokingly fanned himself. They sat down to eat and talked about their days. She told him about how happy the children were to see the pups and the people at the nursing home too. When they were done eating, they put their dishes in the sink and headed out the door to go get some boxes from the store.

When they got to his place, they went and put the boxes in his tipi. "Maybe we should start packing some tonight. We only have tomorrow to get this all done, for the next day will be our wedding," Spirit of Greywolf smiled and winked.

"We can, it's not like there's anything to do at the house. Then we'll load the horses in the trailer and take them to their new home. Do you think they'll like it? "Kiara asked.

"Of course they will. They'll have a new mommy to dote on them…which I'm sure you will," he winked.

"Don't forget I want us to go to that Horse Sanctuary. Maybe the day after we are married, ai?" Kiara asked.

"Ai, it would be nice. It will depend though if you have any strength left in yourself the day after our wedding. I do have plans for you that could very well go on into the wee hours of the morning," he smiled from ear to ear.

"Yes, we shall have to see then if we are not too tired. By the way, when is the next Pow Wow and where? We will probably go to the same ones now right?" Kiara asked.

"We will always go to the same ones K-I-A-R-A. After tomorrow I do not plan on ever letting you out of my sight," he said.

He went over to where he had a stack of papers to look up the next Pow Wow. It would be July 4th through 6th at Rosebud Casino, not too far away. It was right there in South Dakota.

"We have four in August and they are spread out in Oklahoma, Michigan, and Iowa…so we will have to do much traveling if we are to go to all of them. Do you think it would be possible to take all of your wolves if I got you a trailer for your truck so we could just be gone all month and we don't have to worry about anyone watching them? We'll have to take both trucks always because I'll have the horses. Otherwise, I could have put the trailer on mine," Spirit of Greywolf said.

"Yes, I don't see why not. It seems like a good idea instead of trying to come back here after each one. We'd really be pressed for time."

They finished putting the horses in their new corral and they started running around right away. He had built it about twice the size of their old one. He knew they'd be okay. He had put all fresh hay and water for them to drink. Spirit of Greywolf wished them good night and went into the house to be with his Kiara.

32

The following day, after having their coffee and frybread, they left to finish packing up the inside of his tipi so he could take it down.

It was around three o'clock when they were all finished, so he was happy. He told Kiara he'd be able to get the tipi back up by sundown. Then they could unpack everything and she could put it wherever she wanted it to go. He was leaving it up to her. He asked her if maybe they could sleep in it on their wedding night. She loved the idea and agreed wholeheartedly.

By nine o'clock that night everything was completed. They went into the house and had some tea and cake. They talked about the next day, which was their wedding day. He explained to her what she could expect at the Blanket Ceremony.

"I can't believe it is less than twenty-four hours away that you will be my wife. I am so excited. I have never been this excited in my entire life," Spirit of Greywolf said with tears in his eyes.

"I don't think I will be able to sleep either. This all happened so fast! My mind is in a whirl," she said.

"You are not regretting anything are you? If you were to

change your mind I would be crushed. I would follow you to the end of time to be with you again. I will never be able to let you go K-I-A-R-A," he said.

"No, I don't have any regrets and I'm not changing my mind. You have changed my life, Spirit of Greywolf; into something I would have never thought would happen. I have never been so happy. I can't imagine the rest of my life without you now that we have been together. I told you since the first time I saw you that it seems like my thoughts and my life had changed. I can't wait until tomorrow to become your wife forever," she smiled. This time she had tears in her eyes.

He reached over and took her in his arms. He kissed her and said, "This will be your last night alone K-I-A-R-A. Starting tomorrow you will go to bed with me every night…with my arms wrapped around you and wake up every morning with my arms still around you. I will protect you, care for you and watch over you, which is what a man does for the woman he loves. I will worship your body at night and bring you pleasure like you have never known." He kissed her again and said they both better at least try to get some sleep. He didn't want her tired for tomorrow. It would be their first day as husband and wife.

33

The sun shone bright in the sky the next morning. It was very warm outside with a slight breeze. The perfect day for a wedding. Spirit of Greywolf stretched on the couch when Kiara came out of the bedroom.

"Good morning my soon to be wife," he said.

"Good morning to you my soon to be husband," she smiled. She went into the kitchen and put on the coffee. He got up and told her he was going to go check on the horses and the wolves. He wanted to make sure they had enough food and water for the day.

Kiara decided to make them bacon and eggs for breakfast. It would probably be a long day for them. They didn't get to bed last night until after eleven and she didn't know about him, but her head was in such a spin she didn't get to sleep right away. They did finish everything that had to be done in the tipi though, and it looked wonderful. It looked as though it was always meant to be there where it was. As Kiara finished making the breakfast, Spirit of Greywolf was walking in the door.

"Everyone is fine out there. They have plenty of food and water and, of course, they have each other," he told her.

"Good...now sit down and eat. We will need to get to your mother's early. I think she is more nervous and excited than us," Kiara smiled.

Spirit of Greywolf gave her a kiss and told her he loved her and that today was going to be the best day of his life and there was no one more excited than him.

After breakfast they dressed in the clothes they would be getting married in. Kiara had a blue dress with small colorful beads around the neck. It had a handkerchief sort of bottom. She left her long red hair down instead of putting it up like she thought of doing. She looked beautiful.

Spirit of Greywolf had on a tan shirt with a Native American pattern on it and tan pants. He put his hair in a long braid down his back. It had a small feather in it. Kiara had never seen anyone so handsome in her life.

There was a knock at the door. It was Dana from the library. Kiara let her in and introduced her to her soon to be husband.

"Doesn't my soon to be wife look beautiful?" he asked her.

"She always looks beautiful. More importantly, she's beautiful inside for all she does for everyone else," she told him.

They sat and talked for a little while. Kiara and Spirit of Greywolf took her out to show her the new horse corral and the horses and wolves before they left to go to his mother and father's.

When they got there, his mother told them how nice they both looked. She said she was so nervous and excited...you would have thought it was her getting married. Both her and her husband, Chance Two Bears, looked wonderful too. She, like her son, had her hair in a braid.

"Ai, the way this woman has been running around all morning you would think it's her wedding," Chance Two Bears said.

Kiara introduced Dana to Lori Rain Showers and Chance Two Bears. There was a knock at the door and Spirit of Greywolf went to answer it. It was Wild Running Horse.

"Ai, the day is here, Spirit of Greywolf. I told you that you would find this woman of your dreams and make her your wife," he said.

"Ai, she will be my wife and life partner and together we will walk in this valley," Spirit of Greywolf said. He smiled at Kiara.

There was a bustle throughout the house as people came to eat before the ceremony. Tokala and his wife, Wild Running Waterfall, the storeowners were there. Spirit of Greywolf's father, who was a spiritual leader, was going to marry them. They went outside to a place Lori Rain Showers had set up with her husband. There was a sort of trellis that had flowers intertwined throughout the vines. It was beautiful. This is what they would stand under for their marriage.

Lori Rain Showers handed both Kiara and her son a blue blanket. This represented all the sorrows and hardships in their past lives. They each wrapped this blanket around each other. Then came Chance Two Bears, chanting words in the Lakota Language and then in English. He told them how they were now to be comforts to each other. They were to caress each other as they would be caressed. Be a friend and a partner. Be open with each other. Respect each other's rights and allow the other to be an individual. Give each other approval and remember that criticism divides while compliments encourage confidence in each other. He said to cherish your union together, my children. Let no one come between your togetherness. Most of all love one another. Love is your river of life, your eternal source of recreating yourself. Above all else love one another. Then the blue blankets were removed and his mother put a white blanket around both of them together. They wore this for the remainder of the ceremony. They exchanged rings and kissed each other. Then they all walked back by the house where there was much food to enjoy. Even though it was warm out, they built a fire and there was much dancing and talking going on.

Dana was deep in conversation with one particular Lakota named Spirit Moon. He was a friend of Spirit of Greywolf's family. Kiara noticed them and smiled. She had never seen Dana smile so much and Spirit Moon was laughing. She was really glad she had invited her.

At around eight o'clock in the evening, even though everyone was still having a good time, Kiara and Spirit of Greywolf said their goodbyes. It was time for them to retire together as husband and wife as they had planned.

When they got to the tipi and went inside, Spirit of Greywolf started a fire. It was slightly chilly outside since the sun had went down. Kiara was nervous. She had never been with a man, much less one like Spirit of Greywolf. She sat down on a fur that he had spread out by the fire for her. He had put on a cd of Lakota flute music very softly. He gently sat down beside her.

"Do not be afraid K-I-A-R-A. I love you so much I would never do anything to hurt you."

"I know…it's just I have never been with a man and I don't want to displease you in any way. I love you so very much," she said

"You could never displease me. We have our whole lifetime together. There is no hurry for anything between us. We can even sit and talk about our next Pow Wow together if you would like," he smiled.

"No, I want to love you as I want to be loved by you," she smiled lovingly.

She reached over and kissed him gently on the lips. Spirit of Greywolf moaned as he felt himself start to swell. He had never had feelings like this for anyone and to think...this all started from a dream. He felt like he was dreaming now. They lay down on the blanket and kissed each other for a long time. Then he took his shirt off and then his pants. Kiara couldn't help but look at where his swelling had come from. He continued to slip her dress over her head. His eyes devoured her whole body. They came to rest on her perky breasts. He reached over and put another fur around her and laid her back down. His hands cupped her breasts as he rained kisses across her face and neck. Then, much to her surprise he even went farther down to kiss her swollen breasts. He flicked his tongue across each nipple. She could feel his hardness on her leg and could hear soft moans coming from her own mouth. He pulled the fur further over them as he continued to rain small kisses over her stomach. Then she felt his teeth nibbling and she couldn't help but to put her hands on his head and pull at his hair. She felt his wet tongue slide over her most private part, but yet she couldn't stop him or say anything other than the moans that kept coming from her mouth. She had never felt anything like this in her entire life. Then, all of a sudden, her body started to twitch. It was like fireworks going off inside of her. She felt wetness and Spirit of Greywolf's face was opposite hers and she felt hardness where his mouth had just been. He whispered in her ear that he loved her and to tell him if he was hurting her. She felt a push and even though it hurt just a little, it was like she was now complete. Like Spirit of Greywolf and her were now one. She started to match the rhythm that he was moving. She had never been this way with a man and was glad that he was the man she chose to give herself to. His body started to jerk and he lay very still on top of her. It was like time stood still.

After about five minutes he rolled gently off of her. "K-I-A-R-A I didn't hurt you did I?" he asked.

"No, I never would have known anything like this had I not met you," she said.

He took her in his arms and kissed her and told her how much he loved her and he would always make her happy and protect her forever. Then they both feel asleep in each others arms with the fire still going, the music still on and her wolves howling in the distance.

34

Kiara woke the next day to the sight of Spirit of Greywolf lying next to her on his side with his head resting on his hand.

"Good morning mitawin" he said.

"How was your sleep my dear handsome husband?" she asked. She remembered about last night and felt shy.

"I slept wonderfully and I can't help but stare at you, you are so beautiful and wonderful. I can't believe you are now mine. My dream of having you has come true. You are now my wife. After last night I feel more connected to you than I could ever feel to anyone," he said.

She looked down and pulled the fur skin blanket closer to her body. He reached over and with his hand on her face gently kissed each of her closed eyes and then her lips.

"Techihhila so very much K-I-A-R-A. I am so happy we are to start our life together today," he smiled as he kissed her again.

"Do you want to go into the house and I will make you coffee and frybread?" he asked.

"Yes, that would be nice, but I could make it. Why don't you go check on our animals?" Kiara asked.

Spirit of Greywolf got up and got dressed. Kiara watched him as he got up and thought, what a handsome and strong man she had married. His bronze skin was so much darker than her white skin. She didn't care though; all that mattered was their love for each other. She got up and got dressed when he left the tipi after kissing her yet again. When she got into the house, she changed her clothes and then set out to make breakfast.

Spirit of Greywolf came back in and told her that everyone was fine out there. He wanted to know what she wanted to do today, the first day as his wife.

"I'd love to go to that Horse Sanctuary I had told you about," she said.

"That it is then," he said

They finished eating their breakfast and set off for the Horse Sanctuary. They talked about the next Pow Wow coming up. It would be over the fourth of July at the Rosebud Casino.

"Maybe we could go in the casino and play some slots. We might get lucky," Kiara laughed.

"I already got lucky by finding you, but ai, if you want we can go. It will be fun," he smiled.

They got to the Horse Sanctuary and decided to take the three-hour cross-country tour. This was going cross-country in a 4x4 jeep with a guide. They got to see wild horse herds running free. It was a most amazing sight. They went and looked at the wild foals that were for sale. They had Paints/Mediane Hats, Grullas, Spanish Mustangs, Buckskins, Palominos, like Spirit of Greywolfs horses, Roans, Registered Paints and Quarter Horses. Then they went into the gift shop and actually bought three statues that looked like their own horses. On their way back home, they stopped to eat at a small cozy café. They talked about their day and how wonderful it was. When they got home, they went and checked on the horses and wolves. Everyone was fine.

They went in the house and snuggled on the couch. They talked and kissed and hugged until it was time to go to bed. This time they stayed in the house for the night in their bed and did a repeat of last night in the tipi.

35

The following morning was another bright and sunny day. Spirit of Greywolf and Kiara took their morning coffee outside by the table to watch the wolves. Dakota and Denali were playing with their pups...who didn't look so much like pups anymore! Chinook, Maheegan and Makala were all lying down watching them. Kiara had never been so happy! All her great passions were right here with her now. As she looked over at the horse corral, she motioned for Spirit of Greywolf to look. Sunshine and Runs Like The Wind were being chased by their baby Comes At Night! It seemed like everyone was fitting in nicely.

"What do we have to do today?" Spirit of Greywolf asked.

"Nothing really. I need to make sure I have enough of my Black Hills Gold Jewelry to sell at the next Pow Wow. That's about all though," she said.

"Well I believe I will finish some of my paintings. Then we can take them over to Tokala to sell and make some money. He told me on the day of our wedding that he sold another one of my paintings. So when we take these to him he will give me the money."

"Okay, well you do your paintings and I'll see what I need to order. Maybe tonight we can have dinner in the tipi? I really liked staying in there on our wedding night. I wish to do that again tonight if that is okay with you?" Kiara asked.

"Anything you want is okay with me. You don't even need to ask," Spirit of Greywolf said.

He smiled at her with that special smile of his that was reserved only for her. She saw the special glow in his eyes. She knew he really loved her deeply, as he said he did. She felt the same about him too. How was she ever so lucky to have met a man so loving and so attentive to her? She was just happy she did.

They went into the house together. She got out her jewelry and put it on the table in the front room along with her order books. Spirit of Greywolf came walking in with three of his canvases and his paints. He sat at the other end of the couch and started painting. She couldn't help but to watch him. He had such a talent. After a while, it wasn't his paintings she was staring at, but him. He looked over at her.

"I'm not bothering you. Am I?" he asked.

"Oh your bothering me...but not in the way you think," her eyes gleamed.

Right there on the front room floor...you would have thought it was the first time all over again. After about an hour, they were back in seats on the couch doing what they started before getting so distracted.

That night, Kiara made chicken, mashed potatoes with gravy, corn and rolls for dinner. They decided to eat in front of the television and watch a movie and then go retire into the tipi. Kiara had ordered everything she needed for the next Pow Wow and Spirit of Greywolf's pictures were drying so they would be able to take them to sell tomorrow to Tokala.

Around ten o'clock, they retired to the tipi. Kiara had on a little white nightgown with tiny blue flowers down the front. She got under the fur blanket while Spirit of Greywolf started a fire. The night air again had a chill to it, but only until he got under the blanket with her and wrapped his strong loving arms around her. Then, just as their first night together, they continued to love one another as only a husband and wife should do. There were no more dreams for Spirit of Greywolf...because all his dreams had come true. The dreams he had now were dreams they would make together. He was excited for their future together as husband and wife forever and ever through all eternity. What more could anyone want than to find that special someone to share your life with, your hopes and dreams and all your tomorrows. They feel asleep with their arms wrapped around each other, with only Lakota Dreams on their minds.

36

The following day they awoke later than usual. With no windows in a tipi, the sun didn't really come through to wake them. It was after nine o'clock when Kiara went into the house to put on some coffee while Spirit of Greywolf went to check on the animals. When he came back in, she was already dressed and at the stove making him eggs.

"Good morning, my sweet wife," Spirit of Greywolf said. He came up behind her and wrapped his arms around her waist and kissed her neck.

"Good morning to you. Sorry I woke later than I usually do. You must be starving," she said.

"No, I'm fine and besides we don't have much to do today except take the paintings to Tokala to sell," he smiled.

He walked into the front room to check on his paintings to make sure they were dry. As he looked at them, he thought they looked like some of the best paintings he had ever done. Maybe it was because he was so happy with Kiara. As he thought about this, he looked over at Kiara and smiled. He credited all this to her. She was the one that made him happier than he ever thought he could be.

"Here you go," Kiara came in and set his food down on the table. "Your paintings look beautiful. He's going to sell them as soon as he gets them," she said.

Just then the phone rang. Kiara picked it up. "Dana, hi how are you doing?" Kiara asked.

"Fine! How's married life treating you so far?" she asked.

"It is wonderful. I couldn't imagine my life any other way. Is something wrong at the library? Our next presentation date hasn't been changed, has it?" Kiara asked.

"No, everything is fine with next week. I just have a question for you," she said.

"Okay...wow, you had me worried for a minute," she smiled.

"Sorry I just wanted to know a little more about the guy I was talking to at your wedding. His name is Spirit Moon. Do you know anything about him?" Dana asked.

"I really don't know anymore than you. In fact, every time I saw you that day, you were deep in conversation with him, so you probably know more than me! I actually just met him that day. All I know is his family has been friends with Spirit of Greywolf's family for a long time. I could ask him for you. Or better yet, here you talk to him," Kiara said.

"Thanks...he seems like a really nice guy. He asked me to go out with him this weekend and then asked me if I'd like to go to a 4th July Pow Wow with him. I told him I'd call him tonight and I just wanted to make sure he was okay," Dana said.

"Here, talk to Spirit of Greywolf. I'll tell him what you want to know. He could answer your questions," Kiara said.

She handed the phone to Spirit of Greywolf and told him what Dana wanted to know. He got on the phone and told her that he was a good guy. They actually grew up together on the reservation. His parents and Spirit Moon's parents were friends and had been ever since he could remember. They all still lived on the reservation. He had never been married and he didn't have a girlfriend. As for a job, he worked in a little store outside of the reservation that sold Native American items. He also was a dancer at the Pow Wows, like he was and was always hoping to win some of the money.

Dana thanked him for the information. She told him to tell Kiara she would see her next week at the library. She promised to tell her about the date, because she was going to call and tell him yes!

After Dana got off the phone, Spirit of Greywolf told Kiara that Spirit Moon was a good guy and that he thought he and Dana would really get along. Then he told her they should get going with the paintings.

"You never know...someone might buy them today and we'd get to make some money," he laughed.

Tokala was very happy to see them both. His wife, Running Waterfall, came out of a back room and welcomed both of them. Tokala took the paintings and went to hang them on a wall that had three empty hooks from the paintings that sold last week. There was a sign above the paintings that read PAINTINGS BY LAKOTA NATIVE AMERICAN—SPIRIT OF GREYWOLF. Kiara stood and starred at the sign with her heart full of pride for her husband. Then she walked over to a table that had pottery on it. She asked Spirit of Greywolf about one piece in particular. It was a vase with two openings at the top and a handle that connected the two. He told her that was what they called a wedding vase.

"We'll get one if you want," he said. He told Tokala to wrap the vase up she liked and take the money out of what he was getting for the paintings he sold last week.

When they got home, she put the vase on a shelf in the front room. She thought it was beautiful. She wished she could make things like that. She wasn't all that artistic so she really didn't think she could, but she bet that her husband could. They could sell pieces like this at the Pow Wows along with her jewelry. When Spirit of Greywolf came back into the room, she asked him if he thought he could do pottery like the vase. He told her he'd have to get a pottery wheel, but yes, he thought he could. All his life on the reservation he had watched his people make things like this, so he kind of knew what to do. He'd have to start with making bowls though. The wedding vases would take some practice. He told her it was a great idea and maybe she could learn with him. Maybe they could even set up some kind of a little store in front of the house and sell her jewelry, his paintings and the pottery. They were close enough to where all the tourists came to see Mt. Rushmore and The Black Hills. Then they could do the Pow Wows and she could still do the library once a month and the nursing home once a month. He told her he'd like to go with her and help her when she did that too.

    They agreed that tomorrow they would go and get what they needed to start to learn pottery. They ate dinner that night and retired early, even though they had gotten up late that morning...they had some other business to attend to before sleep would overtake them.

37

When Friday morning rolled around, they were both up early. They were excited about going to get all the things they needed to start trying their talent at pottery.

As Kiara was putting sugar in their cups of coffee, Spirit of Greywolf came through the front door.

"Let's see if I can remember all. The horses are Sunshine, Runs Like the Wind, and Comes at Night. All are fed and doing well. Now the wolves they too are all fed and doing well. Let me try to name all of them…. Maheegan, Shunkaha, Mingan, Makala, Mohegan, Chinook, the parents Dakota and Denali and their pups Casey, Kayla, Cailin, Misum and Tacoma. WOW! Did I get all of them right K-I-A-R-A?" Spirit of Greywolf asked.

"Yes, I am so proud of you. Every name was right. Not only are you very handsome…you are also very smart. I do believe you will have no problem with this pottery," she smiled.

They sat down and had their breakfast and talked about going to see his parents on the reservation before they buy the pottery wheel and clay he would need to start making bowls.

When they got to his parents, they were happy to see them

both. His mother was thrilled with the new adventure they were going to start doing with the pottery. Even his father thought a little store by Kiara's would be something good. They sat and ate frybread as usual. His mother would never let them leave without eating her famous dish.

They left there feeling really good about the new journey they were taking. Not to mention feeling stuffed! His mother had told them where to go to buy everything they needed. So they went to the store and the clerk helped them pick out all the things Spirit of Greywolf would need.

When they got home, he set everything up in the little barn and Kiara went in to get them both some ice tea. Chinook and Maheegan were running along the fence when she was going by. "Hey you guys how are you doing today?" she asked them. She put her hands through the fence and they both started licking her. "I guess I'll take you two with me to the library and nursing home next week, because after that we have a summer of Pow Wows to go to so you'll be out on the road a lot," she told them. When she brought Spirit of Greywolf his ice tea, he was already trying out his skills at making a bowl.

"Well K-I-A-R-A, what do you think?" he asked.

"I think it looks really good for someone that has never done this before. What's next? Do you have to bake it in the kiln or paint it?" she asked.

"I have all the instructions here. I have to bake it first, then paint it and then put a glaze on it and bake it again. What color and design should I do?" he asked.

"Whatever you want, but something with blue and gray, since those are my favorite colors," she said.

He put the bowl in the kiln to bake after he put a design of arrows on it. They went into the house and wrote down what he would need to build a small building for them to open a store in.

The day went by so fast. They had gone outside and, with ropes, figured out exactly where they would put the building. From the distance they could see all the wolves playing with the pups. When they saw what Spirit of Greywolf and Kiara were doing, they all ran to the fence enclosure to watch them. It was like they were wondering what was going on.

   Nightfall came and they decided to sleep in the tipi. They hadn't been in there in a few days. Spirit of Greywolf started a fire and they both slipped under the fur throw. He told her stories about the Lakota people as he held her in his arms. They talked about the 4th of July Pow Wow coming up, about the store they were going to open and about their future together. Neither one of them could be happier than they were in this moment. Spirit of Greywolf told her, "Even if we ever get mad at each other and have an argument…it won't be bad…because all of the good times we will have together will more than make up for any bad times we have." They feel asleep in each other's arms.

38

The weekend had gone by so fast. Already it was Tuesday and time for Chinook and Maheegan to be loaded in the truck to go to the library and nursing home. She thought about bringing one of the pups, but decided against it. She was just really tired. Spirit of Greywolf was going to just stay home and work on his pottery and the building. Over the last three days he had made ten pieces and they all looked really good. He was catching on really quick. Plus, in the evenings, he was working on his paintings. He even had the frame of the building up. He told her that while she was gone today he was going to put the walls up, because he wanted the building done before they left for the Pow Wow next weekend.

When Kiara got to the library Dana was waiting outside.

"Oh Kiara I had so much fun Friday night! Spirit Moon was like a dream date. We even got together Saturday for dinner and went for a walk. Sunday he took me to meet his parents and his mother taught me how to make frybread. We went back to my house and he stayed and watched television until midnight! I'm not even sure I wanted him to leave! We're going out again tonight and I think I'm going to go to the 4th of July Pow Wow with him. You're going, right?" she asked.

"Slow down girl! I've never seen you so excited! You're making me dizzy! Yes to your question, we will be going to the Pow Wow. It'll be fun if your there. You could come sit by me while I sell my jewelry and we could sit together while our men dance in the competition. I'm so happy for you, that you met someone so nice. Spirit of Greywolf and I said we'd go to the casino while we're there to play some nickel machines and try our luck. Maybe you and Spirit Moon can go with us and then we could all go to dinner. It would be fun. Are you staying at the campground? I have to stay at the campground because of the wolves," Kiara said.

"Geez, I don't know. He hasn't said where we'll stay. I never even thought of it," Dana said.

"Well, whatever. It'll be fun to have you around," Kiara said.

They went inside with Chinook and Maheegan. It was a new school group so Kiara went through her whole speech about interesting things to know about wolves and then she let everyone see the two wolves. They were all so happy to be able to meet two real wolves. The smiles on these children's faces made what Kiara did all worthwhile. She couldn't think of anything in this whole world she'd rather be doing. At the end Dana told her she'd call her tomorrow to tell her where they were staying.

"Oh my gosh, I didn't even think of that. Will we stay in a motel together? Will I have to sleep in the same bed as Spirit Moon? I've never been with anyone before. What am I supposed to do? What if I do something wrong? Could I break it? Tell me Kiara what to do," Dana was almost terrified.

"Don't worry…it'll all come naturally," Kiara laughed.

"Its not funny! When we kissed I felt a stirring in me like I wanted more. Is that terrible of me? I'm not that kind of girl and he's a Native American…what if they don't do it the same way?" she questioned.

"Oh my gosh, call me tomorrow and quit worrying," Kiara said.

At the nursing home the people were all waiting patiently in their chairs in the recreation room, which is where Kiara brought the wolves. They too, just like the children, had smiles on their faces as soon as they saw them. As usual, Kiara stayed an hour longer than she was supposed to. It was just so hard to leave these people knowing that her wolves had brought such happiness to them, if even for just one day.

When she got home and pulled up to the house, she couldn't believe her eyes! There was a building where only hours ago stood a frame. She should have known when Spirit of Greywolf said he was going to do something he did it. He wasted no time. As she got out of the truck he came running up to help her with Chinook and Maheegan.

"Well what do you think?" he asked.

She looked at the building again and there above the door she saw the sign, KIARA'S TREASURES, underneath it said jewelry, pottery, paintings and beadwork.

"It looks wonderful," she said. She was so amazed she didn't even know what else to say.

"I talked to my mother today and she said she would do beadwork for you to sell. I even already have shelves in there with the pottery on that I have finished. Tonight I'm going to finish two of my paintings and you can put some of your jewelry in there too. We could open tomorrow if you'd like. We're ready to go K-I-A-R-A," he smiled.

"Oh I'd love to! I can't wait to open. This is so exciting!! Maybe your mother could even come and sit in the store to do her beadwork. Then when people come in they'd be able to see her doing it. That would be nice," she said.

They walked over to the building so she could see the inside. There on three of the shelves were the ten different bowls Spirit of Greywolf had made. It looked as if he had been doing them all his life. He already had hooks on the wall for his paintings. She couldn't believe her eyes. It was wonderful. They went back outside to put the wolves back in their enclosure. Then went in the house.

Kiara started making Indian Tacos while Spirit of Greywolf worked on his paintings in the front room, talking to her the whole time. The front room and kitchen were combined in one room, so they could see and talk to each other while being in different rooms. The evening flew by. Spirit of Greywolf finished his two paintings and they went out and hung them on the wall in the store.

That night they lay in bed for hours talking about the store and the Pow Wow coming up this weekend. They decided to open the store tomorrow and maybe even on Thursday morning. There were a lot of tourists here right now, so maybe they'd make some sales. Then of course they'd have to get their things ready to leave by Thursday afternoon.

The Pow Wow was set for Friday, Saturday and Sunday, but they were leaving Thursday night to set up at a campground that was close by. Dr. Eagle was going to take care of the horses and the wolves that weren't going with. Kiara was so lucky to have him as her vet, as well as a friend to help her when she went out on the road for these events. She smiled to herself when she thought of how she knew he loved staying here when she was gone. They both finally fell asleep in each other's arms...so content with the life they were making together.

39

Thursday was here before they knew it. They did open their new store Wednesday and Thursday morning and had just closed so they could get ready to leave. They were both very happy. They had sold one of the paintings and some of the jewelry, along with five pieces of pottery. Not bad for just opening the door! They thought that was a good start.

"When we get back from the 4th Pow Wow, I will have to make up more pottery K-I-A-R-A. I am happy with this store. I believe we will make it a success together. You and I together can make a go of this. We will have a good life together," he smiled.

"I know this too, Spirit of Greywolf. I have this feeling that we will do good together and we will have a wonderful life here with our family," she said.

"We never talked about that K-I-A-R-A. Would you ever want to have a baby?" he asked.

"Oh I meant our family as in my wolves and your horses. I never really thought about a baby," she looked down.

"Oh, I just thought maybe you wanted more," he said.

Just then Dr Eagle pulled up. He got out of his jeep. "Well

hello there Kiara! This must be the husband you've been talking about to me," he smiled. He turned to Spirit of Greywolf as he shook his hand. "Sorry I missed the wedding. There was a baby pony being born that really needed my help that day," Dr. Eagle said.

"That's ok. I understand. You did miss a beautiful wedding though, and my bride was the most beautiful woman on God's earth that day and has been ever since," he winked at Kiara.

"Well what is this building you have here? Looks like the two of you have been very busy," he said.

Kiara and Spirit of Greywolf took Dr. Eagle into Kiara's Treasures. He loved it all, but he especially loved one of Spirit of Greywolf's paintings. In fact, he told them he had wanted the one painting he saw done of an Indian Village that had horses and dogs in the pictures. Spirit of Greywolf took the painting off the wall.

"Put this in your jeep. It is yours for helping watch Kiara's wolves and my horses too. I will introduce you to them," Spirit of Greywolf said.

"I couldn't possibly just take this. I will pay you. Kiara knows I love her wolves as if they were my own and she has been there for me since she moved here when I needed her help," he said.

"No, I insist. Because now you will have our horses to also take care of," Spirit of Greywolf said.

"I will love that also. In fact, let's go meet them," Dr. Eagle laughed.

"Only if you will accept this painting. You can buy the next one," Spirit of Greywolf told him.

"Okay, okay but the next one I do pay for or I won't take it," he said.

Spirit of Greywolf patted him on the back and then took Kiara's hand. They walked over to the corral where the horses were. All three horses came up to the fence.

"This is Sunshine, she is the mother of this little one I named Comes at Night and this is his father Runs Like the Wind," Spirit of Greywolf told Dr. Eagle.

"They are beautiful! You should be very proud of all three, which I'm sure you are. It will be my pleasure to take care of them while you are gone. Please believe me," Dr. Eagle said.

The sincerity Spirit of Greywolf heard in Dr. Eagle's voice made him know that what Kiara had told him about the kindness of this vet and how he loved taking care of her wolves was definitely true. He shook his hand again and said, "I know you will take good care of them, I never had any doubt."

They went into the house and Kiara made them some tuna sandwiches and iced tea while they went over where they could be reached and how long they'd be gone. He knew how to take care of them. After all, he was a vet! Plus he had taken care of them many times before. They told him where they kept the apples for the horses. They were spoiled too and they each got an apple a day.

"Which of the wolves are you taking this time?" he asked.

"Well, I was thinking of taking Dakota and Denali with all five pups. You don't think they're too young though, do you?" she asked.

"No. I think that would be nice. They have to get used to going with you," he told her.

By the time Kiara was done saying goodbye to the wolves she was leaving behind, they were already leaving an hour later than they had planned.

"We should have just taken all of them with us. The way she's acting like we're never coming back," Spirit of Greywolf laughed.

"She does this every time she goes…I'm used to it," Dr. Eagle laughed back.

Finally they were on the road. They didn't have far to go so it didn't matter much that they left later than planned. They had decided to just use Kiara's truck with the enclosed trailer for the wolves. The back of the truck was loaded with Kiara's jewelry to sell and Spirit of Greywolf's costume for the dance competition and of course the clothes they needed for the next three days. They headed onto Hwy 18, which would be a straight ride to the Pow Wow. It was exciting because it was the first Pow Wow they would be going to together. Kiara thought back to the last Pow Wow she had gone to when she had first seen Spirit of Greywolf in his dancing costume. That is also where she met Lori Rain Showers. And to think…here she was today beside her handsome husband. Who would have ever thought this would have happened? She was so glad it had though.

The road wasn't too busy, but Spirit of Greywolf thought tomorrow it would be a lot slower. Many people would be taking this same road to the Rosebud Pow Wow.

They listened to a radio station playing flute music. It was very relaxing and they were so comfortable with each other that not a word needed to be said. They made it to the campground within a few hours. They got their site and set up their tent. Their site was in the back of the campground away from the other campers. Kiara always requested this, since she needed it for the wolves. Spirit of Greywolf started a fire while Kiara checked on her little family who, much to her surprise, were all asleep.

"Do you believe they're all asleep?" she asked him.

"Wow, they must really be tired. Come K-I-A-R-A sit by the fire with me and get warm," Spirit of Greywolf said.

She went and sat on a blanket he had on the ground. They looked up at the stars and talked about what would be going on for the next three days. Of course, Spirit of Greywolf wanted to win in the dance competition again. They talked about the store they opened the other day and how good they did for their first few days. Before they knew it they were both yawning.

"We better get some sleep. We're going to both need in for the next few days," Kiara said.

Spirit of Greywolf took her hand and helped her up and they went into the tent. Sleep came quickly for them, but not so quickly as to not show each other how much they were in love.

40

The next three days were very busy. Kiara sold a lot of her jewelry and her wolf demonstrations were a hit with everyone, as usual. Spirit of Greywolf was in every competition he could be in. Luckily, Spirit Moon was in a different category. Tokala and Running Waterfall were at the Pow Wow too, along with Spirit of Greywolf's parents.

Dana and Kiara went and watched Spirit of Greywolf and Spirit Moon in the arena. They both were very good and, of course, they both wanted them to win a share of the money.

On Saturday night, while Spirit of Greywolf's parents sat at the campsite with the wolves, Spirit of Greywolf, Kiara, Dana and Spirit Moon went over to the Rosebud Casino. They had a lot of fun and went to dinner together while they were there.

Sunday when the winners were announced, both Spirit of Greywolf and Spirit Moon took home part of the prize.

The ride home was a quick one. Spirit of Greywolf and Kiara were both exhausted. It had been a good three-day weekend for them. They had made some good money and had some fun with

Dana and Spirit Moon. When they pulled up to the house, Dr. Eagle was sitting out at the table outside of the wolf enclosure.

"Well hello you two! You both look exhausted. At least tell me you had a good time," he laughed.

Kiara walked up to him and gave him a hug. "We did actually have some fun. We went to the casino. It was exciting to say the least, all those machines and colorful lights. It was really great! My wolf demonstrations were a hit and I sold a lot of jewelry and even two of the vases Spirit of Greywolf made," she smiled.

"Were there a lot of people there? It seemed like everyone from out here went there. It was really quiet out here. Before you ask, your wolves were fine. Your horses too, Spirit of Greywolf," Dr. Eagle said.

"I am so happy to hear that. I appreciate what you did for both of us staying here. I know you always helped Kiara out, but you didn't have to help me," Spirit of Greywolf said.

"It was no problem really. I enjoyed every minute of it. Your horses were great. They are so gentle when they take their apples and that pony of yours is just adorable. Almost as adorable as Kiara's pups,' he laughed.

"Thanks again," Spirit of Greywolf said.

He walked over to the truck to unload the wolves. Kiara and Dr. Eagle followed to help. Dr. Eagle right grabbed Tacoma and hugged him and kissed his head. Kiara was beginning to think that was his favorite since he played the most with him. She smiled to herself. She was so lucky to have met this wonderful man who not only was the vet to her animals, but had also become a good friend that helped her when she needed someone to stay with her wolves when she went away.

They finished putting the wolves in the pen and walked Dr. Eagle over to his truck. Again he thanked Spirit of Greywolf for the painting and told him he was going to hang it as soon as he got home. They waved to him as he drove off and went and checked on the horses before going inside the house.

"I believe we'll sleep in a bed tonight K-I-A-R-A. No tipi tonight. We've had a tent for the last three days," he smiled. They both went and got ready for bed. They were really tired and they fell fast asleep.

41

The following morning they got up later than usual. They had been really tired. They had their coffee and some breakfast, then Spirit of Greywolf told Kiara was going to work on some pottery. They had sold almost everything he had made already! She told him she had to sit down and go through her jewelry too. Even though the next Pow Wow wasn't for a month, they had two coming up that month. Plus, now with the store, she really needed to do some ordering. The sooner she put the order in, the sooner she'd get the order and could stock the store.

He gave Kiara a nice sweet kiss before he walked out the door to go into the store. He had a back room there now where he did the pottery. This way, when the store was open and Kiara was in there so was he.

Kiara sat on the couch and started going through what was left of the jewelry so she could make her order out. It was after two o'clock when Spirit of Greywolf finally came back into the house. He told her he had made about six pieces that were being fired. He was going to have a sandwich and start working on some paintings. He started setting up his easels in the front room. She put a roast in the oven for dinner while she was in the kitchen and made herself a cup of tea. When she got back into the front room, Spirit of Greywolf was already sketching out a picture on one of the canvases. It was of a Pow Wow and he had put a table with Kiara and her wolves in it.

"You sketch fast," she said.

"I've been doing this for years, so I guess it's like second nature. This is a picture of you K-I-A-R-A. How I saw you this weekend and how I always want to remember you. I will always love you and love the life you and I have together. I hope when it is one of our times to go that we will go together so we can walk that journey into eternity as one, like we are now. You have brought much happiness into my life. I can't imagine my life without you. You have brought me much joy. My dreams have all been answered when my mother met you," Spirit of Greywolf said.

He walked over to her and picked up her chin as he gave her a kiss. Then he picked her up in his arms and brought her into the next room where he laid her on the bed. He laid down beside her raining small kisses over her face and neck. To heck with his sandwich, he thought. Who needs a sandwich when you can have this? By the time they came out of the room, the roast was done so his sandwich got put away for tomorrow. After eating they went right back to their bedroom because, after all, tomorrow was another day to get done what they didn't today.

42

The rest of July went by faster than ever. Tokala and Running Waterfall came over one day to see the store Spirit of Greywolf had built. They both were very impressed with the building and the pottery that he was creating. Running Waterfall loved Kiara's Black Hills Gold jewelry. She even bought something for herself. It was a beautiful cross on a gold chain. Then she decided to buy a few pieces to put in her store.

Kiara made lunch that day and they ate outside by the wolf enclosure. They both had fallen in love with her wolves. Everyone who met them did. Tokala wanted to know if Kiara would sell him one of her pups. Of course her answer was no! She could never part with any of them.

The day after they came to the house, Dana and Spirit Moon showed up. They too wanted to see their store and, just like Running Waterfall, Dana bought a few things. She bought a pair of earrings and one of Spirit of Greywolf's vases.

Spirit of Greywolf was really getting good at making pottery and had even tried his hand at a wedding vase. He thought it didn't come out too well, but Kiara thought it was beautiful. She told him to try again, but she was keeping the one he made and putting it in their tipi. All he did was laugh. The two of them had built such a beautiful life together already in such a short time. They spent their days in the store where Spirit of Greywolf worked on his pottery and Kiara tended to customers. In the evenings, they would sit out by the wolves and play with them and then go into the house where Spirit of Greywolf would do his paintings while Kiara watched.

Their store was doing really well. Kiara had to order jewelry twice within the last two weeks. Since they would be leaving in a few days for their next Pow Wow in Iowa, she had to double her order to make sure she had enough to sell.

Spirit of Greywolf had made her four paintings too, because she told him she'd like to sell his paintings at the Pow Wows. Of course, when night fell they still took their turns sleeping in the tipi or the house. But no matter where they went to lay their heads, their lovemaking was extremely romantic and sensual. Neither could get enough of the other and neither could imagine being without the other. They both knew that there was no one out there that could make them feel the way they did about each other. This was all because of Spirit of Greywolf's Lakota Dreams.

43

The morning they were leaving for the Pow Wow in Iowa, it was very warm. Kiara had decided to bring Shunkaha, Chinook, Makala and Maheegan. She knew Dr. Eagle would be thrilled to have Tacoma all to himself.

They got to the campground by early evening and set up camp as usual. This time, since their next one was the following weekend in Michigan, they were going to just leave here and drive to where they were staying and spend a few extra days.

The Pow Wow opened as usual with the opening ceremonies. There were many tribal ceremony dancers, colorful native regalia, and lots of arts and crafts booths with plenty of food booths, too. Indian tacos and frybread had become two of Kiara's favorites.

At the end of the weekend, Spirit of Greywolf won some of the prize money and Kiara had done well in her sales. She thought about how busy they would be when they got home, because they only had a week to replenish what they sold. They would be gone for three weeks in September. They had four Pow Wows to attend. This time they were going to Mount Pleasant, Michigan.

This was the largest Pow Wow. There would be hundreds of dancers; several drum groups and Native American food.

Before they knew it they were on the road again. They were very anxious to get home. It had been over a week and Kiara couldn't wait to see her wolves.

When they pulled up to the house, Dr. Eagle was out there with the wolves. He was in the wolf enclosure this time, horsing around with Tacoma and Cailin. These two had become really close, sleeping together, eating together, and just being together.

"How do," Dr. Eagle said when he saw them.

"I should have known you'd be with Tacoma," Kiara laughed. "I suppose you'll really be glad to be here in another week because you'll have her all to yourself again for three whole weeks," she said.

"You're not taking her? Yippee!" he jumped up.

They all laughed and unloaded the wolves from the trailer. When they went in the pen, they were all running around together and sniffing each other like crazy.

Kiara told Dr. Eagle that since her and Spirit of Greywolf were going to be gone for so long next time, she was going to leave all the wolves at home. She was just going to sell her jewelry and his paintings and pottery.

"That is fine with me. You know I love being with them. I don't know what I ever did before you moved here. I believe the day I met you and your little brood here was one of the luckiest days of my life. I can't wait to get back here next weekend," he said.

44

The week had flown by, filled with ordering jewelry and Spirit of Greywolf working on his paintings and pottery non-stop. When they left, you would have thought they were going to be gone for six months instead of six weeks. They hooked up the trailer even though the wolves weren't going with, since they needed it to put all the boxes in of what they were selling. They decided when they came back they were going to throw their own Pow Wow right out their front door.

Well what a three weeks it was. First they went to the Mankato traditional Pow Wow in Mankato, Minnesota. They camped at a state park. It was next to a babbling brook. On their last night there, they sat outside when it was dark with a fire going just listening to the water.

"I can't believe you are mitawin, my wife. It is so hard for me to believe I am not living in a dream. When I would see you at night in my dreams, you were such a wiwasteka, beautiful woman, but you are even more beautiful than my dreams were. You are beautiful inside which is way more important than the outer shell of a body. I am so happy you agreed to be mitawin, my wife," Spirit of Greywolf said.

"I too am happy to have married you. I also see you as being not only handsome on the outside, but you have a inside that is above anyone I could ever imagine. I will love you throughout all eternity and be ever so grateful that you have decided to walk this journey beside me," Kiara said.

Spirit of Greywolf took her in his arms and kissed her deeply before taking her into their tent for the night to show her just how much he did indeed love her.

The following weekend they were at the Annual American Indian Day and Pow Wow celebration. This was the gathering of the Wakanyeja. This was in Chamberlain, South Dakota at the St. Joseph's Indian School. It again was a successful weekend.

The next morning, they awoke early so as to get a early start on the road. They had some places they wanted to go to before the following weekend. They went to the Lower Sioux Agency, which was a state historic site with exhibits on Dakota culture and the 1862 Dakota War. From there they went to a cave that had a guided tour with a sixty-foot waterfall inside. Then they started to drive up to Ely Minnesota, which is where all the excitement for Kiara was. There was a place called The International Wolf Center, which had excellent exhibits on wolves, a resident wolf pack and interpretive programs. Kiara was in her glory when she got there. She talked to a lady about the wolves she had at home. She wished she would have brought them now for the woman to see. Their place was beautiful though. There was a lot of room for the wolves to roam around.

Spirit of Greywolf and Kiara's last stop that week was to a place called the North American Bear Center. This was a place that had videos and exhibits on bear behavior and live bears in a wooden enclosure.

LAKOTA DREAMS

They made it to their next campground by three o'clock on Friday, but Spirit of Greywolf said that since this was their last stop before going home and they didn't have the wolves with them, that they should stay in a motel for the weekend. It wasn't like they couldn't afford it. They were doing really well selling their things. So they went across the street and got a really nice suite. They ordered some dinner and put the fireplace on, even though it was warm outside. Kiara called home like she did every night to see how her babies were doing…and the horses too. They sat down on a little sofa that was in the room and watched television while eating dinner.

Tomorrow was the United Sioux Tribe Pow Wow. This was in Fort Pierre, South Dakota. After Sunday's closing ceremony, they would be driving home. Kiara couldn't wait to see her wolves. She really missed them. She had never been gone from them this long ever.

45

The day after they got home, they basically rested all day. They were exhausted. The wolves were so happy to see Kiara that they pushed her to the ground and licked her face a million times. Spirit of Greywolf was laughing. You couldn't even see Kiara. The wolves were all on top of her. It was a beautiful sight for him to see how much they loved and depended on each other.

The following day they had everyone over for their picnic. Lori Rain Showers and Chance Two Bears were there with Wild Running Horse. Dana and Spirit Moon were there also, along with Dr. Eagle, Tokala and Running Waterfall. Everyone had a lot of fun and way too much to eat. His parents thought their store was really nice. Lori brought a lot of beadwork for her to sell.

Night feel and everyone went home. Spirit of Greywolf and Kiara stayed outside with the wolves for a while after checking on the horses. They stayed out there until all the wolves had fallen asleep.

The next morning, they got up and started making things again to sell in the store. They basically had sold everything they had within the last three weeks. Kiara had gotten a catalog in the mail while they were gone of porcelain dolls. She called the people and made a deal with them to wholesale them to her for the store. She ordered every Native American doll they offered. Spirit of Greywolf was sitting across from her when she did this and started laughing. When she got off the phone he said, "I better go make some more shelves."

"I'm sorry, I couldn't help myself. We've been doing so well on everything we've been selling. I didn't know which ones to pick and I'm sure they'll sell."

"K-I-A-R-A, how did I ever get so lucky to meet you? There's nothing to be sorry about. I love what you do. Most of all I love that we do it together. I do have some leftover wood and I can build shelves today on the wall behind the counter. That way the dolls will be behind you and no one will be able to be pick them up and possibly break them. Actually, I could paint a picture on that wall of an Indian Village and put little shelves here and there that would hold one or two dolls each. What do you think?"

"Oh Spirit of Greywolf, how did I ever get so lucky to get you? I don't want you to do more work than you have to, but yes that would be beautiful," she sighed.

So they got busy. They both went out to the store. Kiara carried his paints and brushes. He started working on the wall right away. She went out to check on the wolves.

Dakota and Denali were both rolling around on the ground with their pups. They really didn't look so much like pups anymore though. Kayla and Cailin were jumping on Tacoma and Misun and Casey was hitting all of them with her paw. Chinook and Maheegan walked over and joined in. Shunkaha was lying by the tree watching like he could care less. Mingan, Makala and Mohegan started their own little play ring. Kiara stood there watching them. It was such a beautiful sight.

She walked over to the horse corral and gave each Runs Like

the Wind, Sunshine, and Comes at Night an apple. She petted them and talked to them just like she did the wolves. What a wonderful life she had now she thought. She walked back to the store and couldn't believe how far Spirit of Greywolf had gotten on the wall. "Oh it looks beautiful just like I knew it would," she gasped.

"I am glad you like it. I want to please you in everyway that I can K-I-A-R-A. You are my dream girl. You are my soul and my life. Without you I am nothing," he kissed her.

They definitely had become one. They knew each other's thoughts and dreams and could even finish each other's sentences. She helped him clean up the brushes when he was done and they went into the house to have something to eat. Later, they went back out to the store and she helped him put the shelves up. Now when the dolls came they could be put up right away.

That night they were sitting in the front room looking at some books they had gotten from Tennessee.

"Look at this K-I-A-R-A. We need an attraction like this out here in The Black Hills," Spirit of Greywolf said.

It was a giant plastic ball with like another ball inside of it where a person would go. A person was strapped inside and went down a sort of track to the bottom of a big hill. Or one or more people could go in with water inside of it and they sort of sloshed around in it while going downhill. This was a new thing here in the United States called Zorb. It originally came from New Zealand. It was going to be a big hit out here in the U.S.

"We sure have enough steep hills out here and lots of tourists too for them to put one here," Spirit of Greywolf said.

They decided to retire early since they had such a busy day.

"Good night K-I-A-R-A-, mitawin, I love you more than you could ever know," he said as he kissed her.

LAKOTA DREAMS

"Good night Spirit of Greywolf, my husband, it is you that I love today tomorrow and always," she said.

"Ai, but you are my dream come true. I loved you before I even knew you. I started loving you in my Lakota Dreams," he smiled.

It was the smile of a Lakota man, the smile that melted her heart. They both knew it would be awhile before they really retired. There was much loving that needed to be done. They lived each night as if it was their last. Each night their love for each other was renewed. He was her Lakota man and she was his Dream woman. She was his Lakota Dream.

46

The years passed by so quickly. The fun they had together never stopped. Their love for each other grew stronger every day. Every night of lovemaking was like the first time they were ever together. This was one couple that definitely was meant to be together forever!

Kiara continued going to the library to educate children about wolves and to the nursing home where residents' eyes came alive at the sight of the wolves. The wolves loved them unconditionally and the feeling was mutual among the residents.

Spirit of Greywolf would sometimes go with Kiara and sometimes he would stay home to paint and make pottery. He had gotten really good at wedding vases. He even made Kiara a very special one on their first anniversary.

They went to about ten to fifteen Pow Wows per year. They even started going all the way to Wisconsin for their big summer festival. After all, they had Dr. Eagle to watch the wolves.

All their wolves and horses were doing well and their store was a big success. Kiara had added wolf and horse statues to their inventory.

Dana and Spirit Moon were married and had a baby boy they named Chance Meeting.

Spirit of Greywolf's parents actually moved onto the property with Kiara and Spirit of Greywolf. He built them a little log cabin. His mother helped out at the store and continued to do her beadwork. His father helped take care of the horses and the wolves, both of whom he fell in love with, but Chinook was his favorite!

Dr. Eagle was still the best friend anyone could ever have and he came over at least twice a week.

Kiara and Spirit of Greywolf still could not believe their good fortune of meeting each other. It was worth more than all the money in the world. The simple life was the best. The love they had for each other was all they needed. Neither could imagine their life without each other.

Had it not been for the Lakota Dreams that Spirit of Greywolf had, he might never had known what he was looking for. Then he would have never looked for Kiara and he would have lived a lonely life. He thanked God every night for his Lakota Dreams.